The Silent Pool

GRISELDA GIFFORD

ANDERSEN PRESS · LONDON

First published in 2005 by
Andersen Press Limited,
20 Vauxhall Bridge Road, London SW1V 2SA
www.andersenpress.co.uk

The right of Griselda Gifford to be identified as the author of this
work has been asserted by her in accordance with the Copyright,
Designs and Patents Act, 1988

British Library Cataloguing in Publication Data available

ISBN 1 84270 383 8

Typeset by FiSH Books, London WC1
Printed and bound in Great Britain by Bookmarque Ltd.,
Croydon, Surrey

To Jim and the family.

*With many thanks to my editor, Audrey Adams,
and my agent, Pat White,
and for the help of the 'mirror' twins, Julie and Mandy.*

FAMILY TREES

THE TWINS' FAMILY

Reuben Boswell (1873 – 1933) m. Kezra Lee (1876 – 1969)

Rose Boswell (1897 – 1914)

Nathan Farthingdale (1900 – 1938) m. Flora Boswell (1914 – 1979)

Sam Smith (1920 – 1969) m. Kezzie Farthingdale (Gran) (1935 –)

Reuben Smith (Dad) (1959 –) m. Kate Wright (Mum) (1967 –)

Charlie Smith (1991 –) TWINS Cass Smith (1991 –)

CLEREMONT FAMILY

Sophia Johnson (1870 – 1902) m. Thomas Cleremont (1865 – 1915)

James Cleremont (1893 – 1913) TWINS John Cleremont (1893 – 1917) m. Lucy Stones (1896 – 1955)

Elizabeth Fellows (1923 – 1990) m. Robert Cleremont (1915 – 1965)

Alice Foster (1962 –) m. Harry Cleremont (1960 –) TWINS Thomas Cleremont (1960 –)

Jack Cleremont (1990 –)

Chapter 1

CHARLIE

'Are you ready? Dad's waiting in the car,' Cass said. 'He thinks you're packing for the weekend.'

'No – I'm not coming and you can go and drool over the baby by yourself!' I shouted. 'I'm staying here.'

My twin sister went white, so her freckles stood out on the awful pale skin we share with the frizzy red hair and green eyes ('like gooseberries' the nastiest kids say at school).

'Mum will be disappointed,' she said quietly.

'So what? She shouldn't have gone off. And Dad needs me here.'

Gran marched into the room. 'He doesn't need you, Charlotte,' (and I hate being called that. I'm Charlie to nearly everyone else). 'You've forgotten. He's off to a weekend conference when he's left you both at your mother's.'

'I can help you, then.'

Gran's smile smoothed out her craggy face which usually looks like it's carved from stone: she has a jutting chin and big witch-like nose. 'You know what was agreed,' she said quietly. 'Your mother has made her choice but she has a right to see both of you. I may not like her lifestyle but she is still your mother and she loves you.'

1

I looked up at her. I'm normal-sized for my age but Gran is enormously tall, with broad shoulders and muscular legs from all the un-granlike activities she does: going for hiking holidays, cycling, digging her garden and swimming lengths in the local pool with a gaggle of oldies. I wished I could swap her for our cuddly gran, Mum's mother, who went with Grandad to live in America with Aunt Kate two years ago.

This gran, Dad's mother, believes in tidiness and discipline. She said she had to be tidy when she was very young because they lived in a caravan. Gran's mother had gypsy blood; Romany is the right name, I think. Gran has been a widow for years and years and Dad said he could hardly remember his father, who was ill a great deal, which meant his mother ran the shop.

'Go and tell him I'm not coming!' I shouted at Cass and ran out of the kitchen and through the door to the garden. I could hear Gran calling me but I went on, down the path between the neat rows of vegetables and herbs, past her beehive, through the back gate, into the alley between the cottages and then on through the village.

Why was I crying? I'd got out of going to Mum's for the weekend. Dad would be angry with me but I was used to that. I wouldn't be seeing seriously weird Zak and I'd not be kept awake by a bawling baby. Of course I'd get a lecture from Gran but if I kept away from her cottage as much as possible she'd simmer down as usual. We'd only been staying with her a week now, since the beginning of the summer holidays, but I already knew Gran was on

Dad's side and thought like I did, that Mum had gone off her head, leaving him like that. Maybe that's what made Gran so uptight at the moment.

I ran automatically, as if I were practising for the long-distance run at school – which I'd won last year with Cass several yards behind me. I narrowly missed knocking over a very bent old woman dressed in black old-fashioned clothes with some kind of fringed scarf over her head and carrying a wicker basket. I had to stop because she grabbed at my arm with hard fingers. 'Look where you're going! And mind where you're going.' She'd pulled me close to her and I could smell lavender and peppermint. 'Be careful!' she hissed and the whiskers on her chin trembled. 'I see danger.'

I looked up the road in case she meant I was going to be run over by a runaway lorry but there was nothing. The silly old bat was obviously off her head.

I went on running. Then something made me turn round a few paces down the street. The old lady must have scuttled off very fast because exactly where she'd been was another women, younger and ordinary-looking and weighed down with plastic bags of shopping.

I ran on, vaguely disturbed, so I narrowly missed bumping into several tourists who were strolling round, admiring the ancient cottages and drinking on benches outside The Cleremont Arms.

We live at the edge of a big town, in what I always thought of as a boring estate of neat little houses with very small gardens. With Mum gone and Dad going away on business a lot, he felt he couldn't manage to be with us during the summer holidays, even if Mum had us for weekends. I think she'd offered to have us for the whole holidays but as I wouldn't go there, staying with Gran seemed a good idea.

We'd mostly seen her at Christmas or for short visits when I suppose she was on her best behaviour, but in the week we'd been here, she'd turned out to be Granite Gran with all sorts of Rules written in purple ink and stuck on doors and above sinks. ALWAYS WASH YOUR HANDS. REMEMBER TO CLEAN THE BATH and stuff like that. We even had to take our shoes off when we came in and instead of watching TV while we ate, like we did at home, we had to sit round Gran's dining-table and try not to spill things on her hand-embroidered tablecloth. I could see now where Dad got his fussy ways, which didn't suit Mum – or me, really.

Cass loved the tidy cottage and she was allowed to help in the shop Gran ran in the front room, selling honey, home-made jam, marmalade, fudge, lavender bags, guide-books and postcards and, of course, her own bags of herbs. She said it had been a proper shop and Post Office years back but an 8-8 Supermarket and Post Office opened in the village and she couldn't compete with that. Gran wouldn't let me help in the shop after I dropped a pot of honey and managed to jam the till, which could have happened to anyone, couldn't it? It was an old-fashioned till, anyway – no bar codes or anything like that for Gran.

As I jogged along I had a quick sad memory of Mum's oil paint-splattered apron and the brush in her hand, as she painted a canvas propped in a corner of our kitchen at home. She'd get carried away with what she was doing, so bits of paint got stuck on door handles and on the phone. There was always a smell of turps which Dad said made him sneeze.

When we came here, last week, I'd put one of Mum's smaller pictures – of bright poppies in a cornfield – into my bag. She hadn't taken all her paintings to Zak's because there wasn't room, so they were banished to the garage at home, where I used to look at them. I felt if we had her paintings, she might come back one day. Surely Mum could tidy up a bit and Dad could loosen up so they'd get on? I pushed the thought of the new baby to the back of my mind. Or perhaps Dad was really so fond of Mum he'd take her back, baby and all?

Now I was at the edge of the village. Dad could have driven round to find me but I guess he was too mad at me to bother.

Where was I going? It was a boiling hot evening and I could feel my tee shirt sticking to my back. I made off down a tree-lined road, dodging in and out of cool shadows.

At last I was on the crest of the hill, panting hard and looking down at a huge house in extensive grounds. There was a faint glimmer of water.

It was the cool thought of water that set me running down the hill until I came to a pair of large wrought iron gates between pillars with a big stone bird on each side. There was a notice on the gate: **CLEREMONT PARK Open Sundays, 10 – 6. Admission £4. Senior Citizens & accompanied children under 14 £2**. Then there was a notice about a special Edwardian Weekend.

Dad had mentioned the place and Cass asked if there was a Safari Park with lions.

'Lions!' Gran smiled with her lips closed. 'Long ago, there was an eccentric Cleremont who kept all kinds of animals as pets but I believe they're now very short of money to keep the place up – maybe that's why Sir Harry Cleremont disappeared a few weeks ago. He couldn't stand the strain, I guess.' She frowned. 'There's bad blood there. The Cleremonts accused my great-grandfather when he was innocent. And since then, most of the Cleremont men have died violently, before their time.' She paused, thoughtfully. 'Anyway, I don't hold with folk living in great houses while so many people can't afford a proper home. And titles are out of date too.'

'Yes, m'lady,' Dad said, smiling. He could tease Gran and get away with it.

The gates were shut but I went further along the wall where the bricks were crumbling and I noticed a big gap in the spikes protecting the top.

I'm good at climbing. Before the Great Split, Cass and I used to have races up the trees that grew on the Common at home. Sometimes Cass won but more often I did. To be fair, she's slightly smaller than me and has always been the one to catch every bug going. She says

6

it's because I was born first and probably took up most of the room inside Mum, pushing her in a corner so she didn't grow so well.

A car went past and then the lane was empty. I didn't want to be seen trespassing but I knew I had to get inside. Anything difficult always makes me determined to win.

The nails I've not chewed already were broken off as I clawed at the wall, finding footholds where the bricks had fallen out. I climbed through a gap in the spikes and let myself down, not slowly enough because I landed in a patch of nettles.

I swore out loud and great black rooks rose from the trees, cawing wildly, letting everyone know I was there.

I spat on my stinging palms and looked about, for a moment fearful of guard dogs or a gamekeeper, but nothing happened. All I could hear were the pine trees gently soughing in the breeze, reminding me of the sea.

Through the trees to my left I could make out the drive but I didn't want to meet anyone. Then I saw a kind of path to my right, winding through the trees, just asking to be explored. I tried to be quiet but I crunched twigs and pine cones underfoot and the noise seemed loud in the quiet wood.

I came to a fork in the narrow path and as I wondered which way to go, I saw a huge wolf approaching, eyes gleaming in the dusky wood. It growled. My feet were stuck to the ground. It was like one of those nightmares you get when Something is about to pounce and you can't move.

The wolf padded towards me and crouched down, ready to spring. Then I saw that it wasn't grey like most wolves but cream-coloured with strange blue eyes and it was slowly wagging a curly tail. Maybe this was some kind of German Shepherd cross-breed. I was breathing normally again. The dog could bite me but at least it wasn't a wolf.

'All right, boy,' I said, putting out my hand. I liked dogs and so did Mum but Dad said they'd mess up the garden and be a tie so we couldn't go on holiday. So we had two goldfish instead.

The dog came up to me and looked up, hopefully. 'Sorry, nothing for you,' I said. I felt silly – why had I been so scared?

He turned and trotted back the way he had come, stopping to look at me as if asking me to follow.

I ran down the narrow track between the dark pines and saw the water gleaming in the sunshine. The heat and silence seemed to press down on me as I stood by the edge of a lake surrounded by thick pine trees.

A big bird, that I recognised from TV as a heron, admired its pale grey reflection as it stood on the bank of a small island that was a few metres from the edge of the lake. Near a bridge that had once been painted red there was a notice saying PRIVATE.

Suddenly, something startled the bird and it rose into the air on huge wings, its harsh cry echoing round the tree-enclosed water like a warning.

The sun went behind a cloud and a thick mist rose

from nowhere, turning the sunny day to evening. The lake looked sinister and I felt scared.

The dog must have run fast over the bridge because he was barking from a clump of trees on the island. Then I heard faint shouts and a girl came running over the bridge and straight past me, her full skirt almost touching me as she ran into the woods. Her dark hair was coming down from a kind of bun and her black straw hat floated off and landed at my feet.

I told myself the dog had scared her. She looked a bit odd; perhaps she was sleeping rough on the island. Or maybe she worked for the Cleremonts.

At that moment the dog came trotting back over the bridge, his tail wagging. He came up to me and stared at me before turning round and going back again, looking over his shoulder. He wanted me to follow.

The mist had risen and now the sun was shining and even the heron had gone back to sitting on the bank, in exactly the same place. Everything looked so normal that I ran to the bridge and began to walk across the rotting planks. After all, the dog and the girl had gone over it and so could I. At least the handrails were there, covered with the remnants of red and gold paint.

I was watching the dog's curly tail disappear into the thick bushes on the island when I came to a gap in the planks. I jumped too late and too short and fell through into the lake with a loud splash. As the water closed over my head I heard the heron's mocking cry.

Chapter 2

CASS

'Don't worry. I'll make her come with you next time,'
Dad said as he drove me the sixty miles or so to Zak's
house. We were driving back towards our home town.
Zak worked at the local Arts Centre.

I couldn't answer so I looked out of the car window,
not really seeing the traffic nor the countryside. How
could I explain I didn't want him to force Charlie to
come? He didn't seem to understand we'd split up. We
weren't the Twins any more but separate Charlotte and
Cassandra. Charlie doesn't like her full name, by the
way, but I like mine. Mum says there was once a
Cassandra who could see into the future: sometimes I
imagine I can but I try to forget because it gives me a
weird feeling.

When we were younger, Mum used to dress us the
same and we had fun, taking each other's place, even
occasionally fooling people who knew us. We never
fooled Mum and Dad, though, because they know us so
well – they knew about the little black mole on the right
side of my face and Charlie's mole on the left. She's left-
handed and I'm right-handed. Dad says it's called being
a 'mirror twin'.

I believe lots of twins make up a language of their

own and we did too, when we were small. It was fun being Us against the World.

Then we grew up a bit and had different friends. Charlie tore around on her cycle with her lot – mostly boys – and I did quieter things, like dressing-up and acting plays with my friends, who were mostly girls. But we were still the Twins and, even if we fought, we always stuck up for each other. I got sick more often than Charlie and then she was so good to me, sitting by my bed and putting her cool hand on my forehead. I reckoned I used to get better from that moment and we used to joke about hiring her out as some sort of healer.

Then Mum and Dad began to have quiet, icy sorts of rows. There was a nasty tense feeling when you walked in the room and they pretended everything was all right. Mum looked pale and said she hadn't been very well but she still went to her art classes and, once, away to a painting weekend.

The next minute they told us they were splitting up, just like the parents of half our class but we never thought it would happen to us.

That's when Charlie and I split up too. She said Mum was a 'selfish cow' for leaving Dad and she ought to know better than to have a baby at her age, specially as Zak was younger than her. 'It's so gross!' she said.

You'd never think she'd once been close to Mum, who always defended Charlie when Dad got cross at her untidy room and the way she was always losing her school things and not giving in her work on time. Mum and I were close too, but in a different way. I helped her round the house and wiped the oil paint off door handles so Dad wouldn't give her that cold Look. And I backed her up when she wanted to go away on that art weekend. I suppose she was really off with Zak and that's so sad now to think I went along with it.

Charlie went once to Zak's house – after the baby was born – but she didn't like Zak (and she hardly looked at the baby) and she refused to go back. Dad tried to make her because he said Mum had a right to see us but Charlie ran off for the day and hid up in the old grave-yard. I knew where she was but of course I didn't tell.

When I heard about the baby coming I was excited. I like babies and I often wished Mum and Dad would have another child. Dream on, Cass!

He's called Daniel – already we're calling him Danny or Dan – and he's the most beautiful baby you've ever seen, with black hair like Zak's, just beginning to curl, and huge brown eyes. When I got back, that first time, I told Dad how lovely he was and he just said that it was time for bed and he had work to do. So I never talk about him now.

I'm taking Dan a present of a woolly lamb I bought when Gran took us shopping last weekend. She gives me a little pocket money for working in her shop but the lamb cleaned me out for the time being. It will be worth it to see Dan hold it in his doll-sized fingers, tipped with tiny nails like the little pink shells I've got in my collection. He's just beginning to smile and I'm sure he recognises me. Zak's very proud of him and carries him

12

on a sling round his neck all over the place. Mum says she had to stop him painting while he holds Dan because of the smell of oils. Also I think Zak gets so absorbed by his work that he might easily trip over something and squash Dan flat, like a pancake.

Sometimes I hate Charlie for not loving Dan and because Mum always looks up hopefully when we arrive, in case Charlie's with us. I heard Dad saying to Gran something about Mum's lawyer saying she had a right to 'legal access' – which means she has to see us both, and that he'll take Charlie to Mum's even if he has to force her into the car but that won't do any good. I've lost Charlie and so have Mum and Dan.

When I get back, though, I'm going to try hard to make Charlie understand how happy Mum is. We had cameras for our birthday so I shall take photos of the baby. I'm sure she'd love to see him now he's a bit older and gives that lovely smile of his. I love helping bath him and I wish Mum wasn't feeding him herself because I want to give him a bottle feed, but Mum and Zak are very keen on the best for Daniel, which means only Mum can feed him.

Dad's hardly said anything on the journey – I expect because he's still mad at Charlie – so I asked him to put on one of his classical tapes. I like pop music best but that wouldn't put him in a good mood!

Now I can see we're coming to the village and there's Zak's tumbledown house with its crooked chimney and the big barn where he paints. I'm so longing to see Mum and hug her and look at Dan. I just can't wait!

13

Chapter 3

CHARLIE

Of course I can swim, unlike poor Cass who's scared of the water and after masses of lessons does a couple of strokes and then keeps her toe on the bottom. When nobody's looking she puts on babyish armbands as well.

I swam to the island and pulled myself up the muddy bank by a tree root. My clothes clung uncomfortably to me and I was cross with myself for falling in.

A narrow path led through the bushes ahead and I thought I saw the dog's tail and rump, just ahead.

I came to a small clearing almost filled by a dome-shaped building, made of marble or something like that. I recognised it as an old-fashioned kind of family tomb, the sort that has a door and I suppose places inside for everyone. Though I often wondered what happens when it's full up. Before the Split, Cass and I liked to wander in the old part of the town cemetery, reading the inscriptions or just lying in the long grass looking at the sky and pretending we lived in the country. Mum said those big tombs were called mausoleums.

I whistled but the dog didn't come. It must be hiding in the bushes somewhere. I wandered round the mausoleum, wondering if you could get inside, if you dared.

There were words carved round it, some a bit mossy, but I read while walking round the monument:

Lady Sophia Cleremont. Beloved Wife of
Sir Thomas Cleremont
Born 1870 Died 1902
Rest in Peace

Then there was a kind of shield carved with two birds like herons, necks entwined and something in French underneath: *Verité sans Peur.*

I'd done a bit of French. I'd forgotten the first word but the last two meant *Without Fear*. Must be a family motto or something like that.

Stone steps led down to a door but it was shut. I went down the steps and pushed but it didn't budge.

Suddenly I felt fear and sadness, like a dark cloud that swamped me so thoroughly I sank down on the step.

This had happened to me before, often just a shadow of cold sadness and a strange feeling when our school had been taken to places like the Tower of London and once, at an old mill where people were wearing Victorian dress. I'd asked a mill girl why her face was bruised and she'd cried. The teacher had called my name and when I turned round again, the girl had gone. I know actresses played the Victorian parts but surely they didn't cry real tears? Cass says for films and TV they rush out with onions but Dad laughed (yes, he used to laugh a bit) and said he didn't think it was quite like that.

The time I remember most was when we'd been on

holiday and visited the dungeons in an old castle. Cass had gone pale too but she pretended to be bored, saying she wanted to go to the tourist shop. I knew she felt the same as me but she never admitted it. In fact, she laughed at me for saying the place had a terrible feeling. That's how she is, all cheerful and calm on top but different underneath. She says I'm a Drama Queen but she's one long act herself lately. The real Cass has been buried under a layer of gooey niceness. You'd think Mum's running off and having a baby was the best thing that had ever happened to her. She'd guessed about the baby even before Mum told her, when it must have been as big as a pea. Cass sometimes knows what's coming but it scares her.

Anyway, there had been a few other times when I'd felt on the edge of another world – not all sadness and fear, though. In fact, I heard laughter more than once but of course it could have been from someone out of sight. I couldn't explain it and after Cass laughed at me I never talked about it to anyone. It was yet another thing we might have shared once but not now.

As soon as I moved away, I felt fine. I sat on a flat, mossy stone in a patch of sunshine and thought this would be a good place to get away from Gran's fussing and Cass's soapy smiles.

Judging by the broken bridge, nobody came here except the dog and that girl: the dog could have jumped across the gap but the girl? And maybe the dog was a stray and I could tame it if I brought food. I whistled again

16

but it didn't reappear and I suppose it had gone back, through the bushes and over the bridge or swum across.

There was a short path opposite to the one that led to the bridge and I could see the lake gleaming in the sun. Beyond the trees, I could just see the big house. So if I wanted to hide, I needed to find a place in the bushes.

Pushing through the thick undergrowth and young trees swathed in cascades of sweet-smelling honeysuckle, I found a very small tumbledown shed, the roof so low that I had to stoop. Inside were rusted gardening tools. Probably years ago, the island had been planted with flowers and kept tidy. There was even a broken stool and an old box to sit on.

I looked at my watch – luckily it was waterproof – and realised that Gran's anger with me would be much worse if I missed supper. I decided to come back to the island as soon as possible.

I swam the few metres back to the shore. As I ran back through the wood I thought I heard the dog barking again and someone shouting. Perhaps it was someone from the Park. Just as well I was going.

I tried to get upstairs to change when I got back but Gran must have heard me. She ran up the stairs, calling me. 'Charlotte! Why are you wet? And where have you been?' she snapped. 'Your sister rang you.'

I didn't tell her, of course, and as a kind of punishment she made me help get supper (shelling hundreds of boring peas). Well, actually she said, 'I could do with some help, Charlotte,' but I knew I had to do it. Then we

17

put bunches of different herbs into little bags for the shop. She's got a minute black and white TV but there was no time to watch that. *And* I had lectures about not going to see Mum, of course. 'You're upsetting her, you know,' Gran said. I didn't answer.

It was just as bad next morning. I'd planned to go back to the island but Gran was still so cross that I was forced to help her round the house, hanging out washing, tidying my side of our room – at least at home we had a bedroom each – and even digging up potatoes, while she served in the shop. I kept well away from the beehive and the very active bees, who were dashing in and out, sometimes buzzing near me.

I was feeling thoroughly cross and sweaty when a voice said, 'Are you Charlotte or Cassandra, dear?'

An old man was peeping over the tall hedge. He must be standing on a ladder. His lined face was tanned leathery brown, even the top of his head because he was as bald as an egg. His eyebrows were so shaggy that his blue eyes peeped out as if under a fringe. 'I'm your gran's neighbour and friend, Freddy Farthingdale.'

I nearly giggled but I said, 'I'm Charlie.'

He smiled and all the lines went upwards. 'Very pleased to meet you. Please tell your gran that I have something for her. And that her ointment did wonders for my back. I'd like to buy some more.' He paused and what I can only say was a dreamy, soppy look came on his face. 'She's a wonderful woman. There's magic in her hands.'

Then he disappeared down the ladder. So Gran had

18

an admirer – at her age! He'd said, 'magic in her hands' – had she been giving him a massage or what? I thought it would be fun to giggle with Cass about this on Sunday night but then, she'd come back full of boring baby-talk which turned me right off. And we didn't giggle together now.

I was glad of an excuse to stop. I threw the potatoes into the trug, washed my hands and went to give Gran her message.

An oldish woman was looking at the postcards and guidebooks while her husband stood by. I could feel Gran's impatience because another couple was waiting for their turn, holding pots of honey and marmalade.

'Look, Norman!' the tourist said. She had an American accent. 'This is just so romantic! There's a photo here of the island and the pool at Cleremont Park. We just have to go there. Listen, honey.' She began to read aloud: '**From the side of the lake, called by the locals The Silent Pool, you can just see the top of a mausoleum built in 1902 for Sophia, Lady Cleremont, the beloved wife of Sir Thomas Cleremont, who drowned in the lake. There are different accounts of why she was buried there instead of in the family vault at St. Martha's church; some say her husband was so overcome with grief at her accidental drowning that he built a special mausoleum for her. There were also rumours that she fell in the lake as she was running away to meet a lover and Sir Thomas felt she was unworthy to be buried in the family vault . . .**'

19

'Oh, the poor girl!' The tourist looked quite upset. 'It sounds just like Lady Diana. You remember, Norman?' He grunted. 'She's buried on an island at her childhood home.' She flipped through the pages. 'And here's something else: **There is a legend that there is a curse on the Cleremont family that none will die in their beds. Lady Sophia's twin son mysteriously disappeared at the age of twenty and his brother John was later killed in the Great War. A gypsy...**'

Gran interrupted with a flinty smile: 'Cleremont Park is only open on Sundays and I believe the island and mausoleum are forbidden to visitors. The guide book costs fifty pence,' she added pointedly.

When they'd gone and Gran had served the other people, I passed on Freddy Farthingdale's message. She nodded, looking as pleased as Granite Gran could: 'I treated him with my horseradish embrocation. He's like all men – can't bear a bit of pain. I reckon he wants to off-load his bolting lettuces on me.'

I wanted to giggle again, thinking of bolting lettuces running out of the garden on tiny green feet. Then I remembered what the tourist had read out. I had to be careful what I asked Gran in case she guessed I'd been to the island.

'Is that story true – about the legend and the deaths and stuff?' I asked.

I couldn't see Gran's face because she was stooping to get replacement jars of marmalade from the bottom shelf behind the counter. 'Oh, you always get all that nonsense with an old house. It helps bring in the tourists.'

Or the casual trespassers, like myself and the girl I saw running, I thought.

How could I get away from Gran and back to the island – *my* island?

Chapter 4

CASS

Mum allowed me to bath Dan by myself – with her watching. I was nervous at first because he seemed so small and slippery but Mum showed me how to hold him and how to test the water so it was just the right heat. She said I managed very well and it was the first time Dan had splashed his hands a bit and smiled. Usually he cried a bit when she bathed him.

Zak's cooking one of his gorgeous-smelling curries and the smell fills the whole house. Charlie loves curry more than I do. I wish she were here. I know, I'll ring her while Mum's tidying up the tiny nursery with its exciting jungle-paintings on the walls – done by Zak, of course.

I've brought my mobile and I've got Gran's number in the address book already. I've tried Charlie's mobile but it's switched off.

Perhaps if I talk to Charlie and tell her about bath-time and the way Dan is beginning to smile at me and that Zak's going to get a dog and a cat because he wants Dan to grow up with animals – then she might be a tiny bit jealous and want to come next time.

'She's not here, Cass,' Gran says. 'In fact, I'm cross with her. She's not back yet. She might show some consideration.'

How can I calm her down? 'She'll be fine. Don't worry,' I say. 'She's quite sensible (that's a bit of a lie) and it's light for a while yet. She always has liked exploring.'

I remember Mum going bananas because Charlie had a brilliant idea of going down to the canal that runs through our town and hitching a lift on a boat. Of course nobody wanted to know except a weirdo woman with a very tatty boat and two fierce-looking dogs who said she'd take us up to the lock. I said what about all that 'stranger-danger' stuff we were taught at school but Charlie told me not to be such a wimp and she made me jump on board. She changed her mind when the weirdo woman's strange-looking man emerged from the cabin, offering us dope to smoke and cans of beer. I wondered afterwards if he hadn't smelled and looked odd, whether she'd have stayed because she likes adventures, much more than I do. I'd have jumped off anyway, before they started the engine.

'She'll be all right,' I said feebly now to Gran. 'Tell her to give me a ring on my mobile. I've got something to tell her.' Charlie was always curious and she might very well ring back.

'I thought we'd go to the beach on Sunday. If we leave after tea we should be back in time for your dad to pick you up,' Zak said as he heaped my plate with far too much curry. 'That's if Tilly can make it.' Tilly was his ancient car. 'It's hot enough for swimming. Dan and I

23

can rest in the shade while you two prance in the waves! I might even paint a little if Dan lets me.' He grinned, his teeth very white against his olive skin. I really like him because he gets all enthusiastic and excited about things.

I can't help thinking he's quite different from my dad who's difficult to please and a bit too keen on finding fault. Then I feel guilty.

Chapter 5

CHARLIE

Gran was round seeing Freddy Farthingdale when I slipped off after tea, this time wearing towelling beach shorts and a thin shirt. I hoped they'd dry off quicker than jeans. I left her a note, propped up against her home-made loaf. *Just having a look at the village. Back before dark. Charlie.*

After all, what could happen to me?

It was just as hot but the sun had disappeared behind a bank of coppery-coloured clouds by the time I climbed the wall again and walked through the wood. I'd got a couple of Gran's oatmeal cookies in my pocket and a piece of cheese ready for the dog. I whistled, but he didn't come.

It seemed to grow darker as if a storm were coming any moment.

The crows clattered out of the trees and suddenly I saw a man running along the bank in front of me towards the island. I don't think he could have seen me and I only had time to see he was carrying something in his hand when he ran over the bridge and into the bushes on the island. The heron rose from the bank with a loud cry.

I stood, uncertain what to do. I felt angry that he was

going to my island. Was he perhaps some kind of gardener who had been told to tidy the island for the tourists? But they'd have to mend the bridge first! He obviously knew where to jump across the gap in the middle.

I'd not noticed his clothes, except he had a white shirt that had come untucked so the tails flew behind him. Maybe he'd heard that the girl was back, camping on the island, and he'd been sent to tell her off.

I suppose the sensible thing was to go back to Gran's. But I so wanted to find the white dog again.

As if on cue, I heard barking and growling from the island.

As I was wondering what to do, a shaft of sunlight came through the thunderclouds and shone on the lake. I saw a dog swimming in the lake, round the end of the island. For a moment I thought it was the wolf-dog but it had long spaniel ears. Then I saw another spaniel swimming beside a boy, whose arms lifted in an easy crawl. The dogs climbed up the bank a few yards away and ran to me, wagging not just their tails but their whole bodies, showering me with water.

The boy followed them. He wore ragged, cut-off jeans and water glistened on his bare brown back. 'You're trespassing,' he said in a voice which started low but ended higher.

'What about you?' I snapped. 'And the man who's just gone on the island.'

'What man?'

It almost seemed unreal now the sun was out and even

the heron was back, standing in exactly the same place as if he'd never flown away.

'I saw him – running over that bridge.' I pointed. 'And yesterday...' I was going to tell him about the dog and the girl.

The boy interrupted impatiently. 'I've just swum past the island from the other side of the lake. Didn't see anything. But I'd better look. We've had trouble here before. People trespassing to see the tomb.' He stared at me angrily. 'You'd better go home too.'

'Who are you to be so bossy, anyway?' I said but he was off, jumping into the water with the dogs at his heels, swimming beside the bridge to the island.

I was angry at being told off like that. I plunged into the water after him, doing a show-off dive from the bank. Unfortunately I hadn't realised how much weed there was and I came up clawing it off my face.

The boy and his dogs were sitting on the bank, all laughing at me. 'Help her!' he said to the dogs, waving his arm. They jumped in and I had to fend them off while I swam the few strokes to the island. I almost turned back, I felt so mad at him but I wanted to prove I'd not imagined the man.

I spat out water as I hauled myself up the bank. 'They ought to repair that stupid bridge then you wouldn't have to swim,' I said, horribly aware that my wet tee shirt was clinging to me and he was staring. I wasn't wearing a bra, either.

'*They* haven't any money to spare,' he snapped. He

called the dogs to heel and walked up an overgrown path through thick bushes. 'Better find this man – if he exists,' he said.

He gave an order to the dogs and they went off into the bushes, growling impressively. The boy was only a bit older than me and I suddenly felt nervous. If the man was a poacher or something he could have been carrying a gun and the dogs weren't exactly large and threatening.

Perhaps *my* lovely cream dog would hear them and come out of hiding.

But he didn't come.

We came to the mausoleum and the boy ran off down a thin path through the bushes. Looking straight ahead, you could just see the other side of the lake and a bit of the big house above some trees. The island was so small that nobody could stay hidden for long. Unless the man was hiding *in* the tomb?

The boy came back saying, 'I knew you made it up,' in a nasty voice.

I'd show him! The man must be in the tomb itself. I tried to ignore the sadness clawing at me as I went down the steps and pushed at the thick wood, reinforced by rusty iron bands, but it didn't budge. There was a lock but no key.

The boy was laughing again but I put my ear against the wooden door. I swear I heard a faint cry... 'Help!'

My legs crumpled and I had to sit down on the last step. The spaniels were there, nosing at me with wet sympathy. 'What's wrong with you?' the boy said irritably. 'And there's nobody on the island. Of course you made it up so I wouldn't tell you off for trespassing.'

'I think there's someone in the tomb,' I said.

'Noises in your head, more like! It's been locked for years and years.'

I felt angry that he didn't believe me and stood up. As soon as I walked up the steps, away from the door, I felt perfectly normal and began to wonder if he was right. How could anyone be locked in the mausoleum? 'I'm not making it up. I did see a man, running. He was carrying something.'

He looked a bit more friendly. 'You probably saw the gardener's son, Carl. He likes fishing in the pool – sometimes I go with him. But he'd not go on the island.'

I sighed. Obviously he wasn't going to believe me and perhaps I had imagined him running over the bridge. Well, I wasn't going to tell him about the girl or he'd think I was a right weirdo.

'There was a dog, too,' I said. 'Creamy white with a curly tail. At first I thought it was a wolf.'

He frowned. 'Probably a stray. It might be descended from the Huskies that were once kept here. There were four, including an albino. When it snowed, they pulled a sledge in the park. They say the albino dog, Wolf, used to get out into the village and mate with local bitches. You sometimes see dogs a bit like him around here.'

It had been growing darker and now thunder rumbled

and suddenly rain fell like a solid curtain. 'Follow me!' the boy shouted.

He led me to the hut. I didn't dare say I'd been there already. Once the dogs were inside with us, there was hardly room to turn round. I sat on an old box and one of the dogs put her head on my foot. She was shivering. 'Poor old Merry – she gets scared. No good as a gun-dog,' the boy shouted over the storm. 'The other one, Magic, doesn't mind a bit.'

The lightning flashed through a small window. He pulled a grey-looking towel from a black dustbin sack. 'Towel,' he said, throwing it at me. It smelled of mud and dogs but I rubbed at my hair anyway.

'How did you get that here?' I asked. 'By boat?'

'No. That's fallen to bits. I trod water and carried it in the bag above my head.'

He fetched out two Snickers bars and the dogs sniffed hopefully, smelling the chocolate. 'Like one? I'm Jack, by the way.' Suddenly he was much more friendly.

'Charlie.' I'm always hungry so I bit into the Snickers bar. I thought I might as well be friendly and find out more about the mausoleum.

'You staying in the village?' He had to shout because of the storm.

'We're with my gran at Elder Cottage. She has a shop.'

'I know it. I've heard she heals people with her herbs.'

I couldn't imagine Granite Gran healing anyone but she'd obviously helped her admirer, Freddy. 'Where do you live?'

I think he said, 'On the Estate,' but I couldn't hear because the storm was so noisy.

'I suppose you climbed over the wall,' he said when the thunder died down.

'I just wanted to explore while I could. While my sister Cass is out of the way.'

'So you don't get on?'

'We used to but Mum left us for her art teacher and Cass is on her side and I'm on Dad's. And now Mum's had a baby.'

'Sounds difficult. And I used to wish I wasn't an only!'

'Why do you come here?' I asked him.

'I'm looking for something. And I want to get away too. My father's . . . ' He hesitated. 'Gone away. And my uncle's come to stay. He's keen on my mother. He wanted to marry her ages ago but my father got there first.'

I didn't want him to be unhappy but I suddenly didn't feel so lonely about Mum and Cass. 'Parents mess us up, don't they?' I said.

'Yeah.'

I looked at my watch. It was half past seven and Gran must be back by now. I'd better get back.

The storm was dying down. 'Got to go,' I said. Then I thought he wasn't so bad, really. It would serve Cass right if I had somewhere secret to go to when she got back. 'I'd like to come back – and help you find whatever it is.'

'If you like.' He didn't sound that keen but when we were outside he said, 'Why not? You might have some ideas. The biggest puzzle of all, I can't solve, though.' Then he looked at me as if he wanted to remember my face. I saw that his eyes were a vivid blue with thick black lashes. 'Now that ginger frizz is drying I know I've seen you before, ages ago.'

I decided to ignore his remarks about my hair. There wasn't anything rude I could think of quickly to say about him: he had curly hair that was springing up now it was drying. I suppose he wasn't bad looking.

'We've only been to Gran's a few times before now,' I explained. 'And then just for a night because she hasn't much room. I'm sharing a tiny room with Cass as it is. Gran comes to us for Christmas usually.'

'It was Christmas I saw you. About three years ago. I was in the choir then. But I didn't see a sister.'

I remembered. Gran's old car had conked out for good so we came to her that time, just for a night. That was the Christmas Cass had a bad cough and stayed in bed but Gran took us to church. Mum, sitting beside me, smelling of the flowery scent Dad had given her and wearing my present, a vivid red and blue scarf to go with her red jacket. Dad sat on her other side, next to Gran. He looked bored. We still had stockings then, bulging with little presents Mum had wrapped up. Dad had fussed about the wrappings and ribbons all over Gran's floor but that Christmas he and Mum kissed under the mistletoe. I never saw them kiss properly again – just pecks on the cheek.

'Cass was ill,' I said shortly, hating the memory. 'See you.'

32

I swam back to the lakeside, wondering how I was going to explain being wet again. I turned to look. He waved at me and I waved back, feeling for the first time for ages, just a bit happier.

Chapter 6

CASS

We've driven quite a long way to the seaside – to our old holiday place that Charlie always called Shipwreck Bay because of the skeleton timbers of an old boat that showed up at low tide. I suppose some of those holidays it rained but I can only remember sunny days when we'd get up early from our bunk beds in the living-room bit of the caravan and run down to the Bay before the other campers were awake. Everything seemed to sparkle, dew in the egg-yellow gorse, sun on the sea and the whole lovely long day lay ahead.

I pretended I didn't mind that Charlie learned to swim quickly but I think maybe I got scared because a wave pushed me over when I was little. Of course Charlie pulled me out of the water. She was always the stronger of us two, even then. Dad said since it was so shallow I couldn't have drowned but it put me off. Now I swim a stroke, then I sort of panic and my toe finds the bottom of the pool. Charlie takes after Dad, who's good at swimming and most sports but Mum only goes in the water when it's boiling hot and never goes out far. I used to hate seeming so feeble, even at beach cricket when I always managed to drop catches and I envied Charlie, who doesn't have to make an effort.

Zak's friendly and he says I'm really brilliant with baby Dan. Zak makes me laugh; he's got a mass of silly jokes and he notices if I feel left out, like when I catch him and Mum holding hands. He smiles and says things like, 'Sorry, Cass, your mum and I are still at the soppy stage,' and puts his free arm round me so I feel safe, and included.

After the picnic, Zak and Dan went to sleep in a little cave and Mum began to sketch with her messy charcoal pencils. She got me to sit on a rock wearing a floppy straw hat to shade my face. Charlie and I have to wear masses of Factor 25 and keep out of the sun because we peel like mad otherwise.

I knew she was going to talk about Charlie and she did. 'I wonder how Charlie's getting on,' she said, peering at me over her sunglasses. 'Do you think she'll come with you next time?'

I felt so sorry for her that I hated Charlie for staying away. 'I'll talk her round,' I said. 'She's bound to get bored staying with Gran.' Then I thought that wasn't very tactful. It sounded as if she might only come if she was bored. 'She used to love it here.' I shut my eyes against the glittering sea, trying to imagine Charlie here again but I just had a weird vision of a girl running in fear through a wood. I opened my eyes quickly to get rid of the bad feeling.

'Do you think she misses me?' Mum asked in such a quiet voice that I hardly heard it against the slap of water on the rocks and the cries from the children further down the beach.

'Of course she does.' I'd caught a whiff of sadness from her when she looked at a photo of Mum and baby Dan that I'd put in our bedroom but she'd not said anything.

Mum did a bit of fierce shading with the charcoal. She already had a black smudge on her nose. 'I hope you both try to understand your gran. She's got a kind heart but I think she's had to hide her feelings, long ago. You know she's got Romany blood and I think that meant she was teased at school and sometimes given the cold shoulder later on, when she was older.'

I knew all about that. If I'd not had Charlie to defend me at school I'd have been teased a lot because I'm just the sort that gets picked on. 'I like Gran, anyway,' I said. I nearly said I liked her tidy ways but that would hurt my untidy mum. 'It's fun helping in the shop,' I added. 'Mum, my bottom's getting numb on this hard rock!'

She laughed and I jumped down.

When he woke up, Zak drew a huge picture of a mermaid in the sand and I added fish and seaweed. Mum was feeding Dan in the cave and suddenly, I felt really happy.

Then I remembered all those times here with Dad and how he and Charlie would make sand bridges and motorways and I'd add little sand houses, decorated with shells. Was Mum happy then? I tried to think back through the layers of time. I could only remember clearly the last, unhappy holiday and the angry whispers in the caravan.

36

Dad came to collect me when we got back from Shipwreck Bay. I had Dan in my arms, wrapped in a towel. I heard the car arrive and Zak answering the door. Mum went all tense and called out that we wouldn't be long. I wondered if Zak and Dad would hit each other or something but when I came down, Dad had gone back to the car and Zak was waiting in the hall, looking uncomfortable.

'You should've come to see the baby, Dad,' I said as we drove off. Of course I knew at once I'd said the wrong thing.

'I'm not much of a baby-lover, Cass,' he muttered, frowning at a driver who had cut in front of him.

'Zak offered to bring me back,' I said. 'But I knew you were coming.'

'I don't want that man arriving at Gran's because it will upset her.'

I guessed that Dad himself didn't want Zak turning up. 'Was the Conference fun?' I asked tactfully.

He smiled. 'Not exactly fun but it went well.' He told me some funny story about a special sales video going wrong; he wasn't as funny as Mum could be telling a story because he always had to get all the details right and it took too long. But at least he wasn't thinking about Zak and the baby.

But right in the middle of his story, I knew Charlie was in trouble. Her fear filled me, so much that Dad asked me if I was all right. 'You've gone so pale! Do you think it's a touch of sunstroke?' He sounded quite anxious.

37

'I'm all right but I'd like to ring Gran. I'm worried about Charlie.'

He frowned. 'So am I. She's behaving so badly. But I suppose you've got one of your twin-twinges.' That's what he used to call them, in the past. 'I should ring if you're worried.'

Charlie's mobile was switched off, which wasn't unusual. She'd probably lost it again or left it somewhere. I rang Gran, who sounded cross.

'I don't know where she is. I came back and she'd gone out. So thoughtless. And I can't find the cat, either. She's been out all day. Most unusual when it's hot.'

Then her voice broke up and I lost the connection.

'Charlie's out somewhere,' I told Dad.

'Tell me something new,' he said. 'Women drivers!' and he tooted angrily at the car ahead of us, holding up the line of traffic.

I just had to hope Charlie would be all right.

Chapter 7

CHARLIE

Gran's cat Flora woke me by gently batting my nose with her paw. She seemed to like sleeping on my bed best and I think Cass was just a bit hurt.

It was Sunday and Gran made me come to church with her. We just go at Christmas and Easter at home but Gran seemed to take it for granted I was coming. I thought if I gave way now she'd let me go off later so I changed into clean jeans and a fairly clean tee shirt. Even so, she looked at me. 'Jeans, jeans, jeans!' she exclaimed. 'And you could look so nice in a summer dress.'

'I've only got my school dress and that's too tight,' I said. 'Everyone wears jeans now.'

'I suppose so.' She was wearing a dazzling white shirt and a pleated summer skirt that seemed all wrong with her muscular brown legs and big feet. I was used to seeing her in men's trousers or shorts – she said they'd belonged to her husband, Sam, and she didn't want to waste them.

I was ready to be totally bored but a woman and a boy, tidily dressed in grey trousers and a white shirt, came up the aisle. He winked at me. I felt a jolt as I recognised the boy I'd met on the island! I felt cross.

His mother wore a smart summer suit and had

shoulder-length fair hair – the sort you see in shampoo ads – but she looked pale and sad.

The Vicar was smiley and youngish and I actually listened to a bit of her sermon which seemed to be about having hope even when dreadful things happened. Could you have hope when your parents split up? I hoped they'd get together but I really knew they wouldn't. So was hope like wishes and no real use at all?

Gran nudged me because I was biting my thumbnail so I forced my mind back to the island and the mystery surrounding it. Then I was jolted awake by the Vicar asking us to pray for the safe return of Sir Harry Cleremont.

When we were going out of the church, I heard the Vicar talking to the boy's mother. 'Any news?' she asked and the woman shook her head. 'We mustn't give up hope, must we, Jack?' the Vicar said kindly. Jack mumbled something and looked away.

With a jolt, I realised Jack and his mother must be the Cleremonts and own the Park.

Gran looked sad as she marched down the path, nodding at people she knew. I felt a touch on my shoulder. 'Hi, Ginger!' Jack said. 'See you!' and he ran ahead of his mother, out of the gate. I suppose it was because he didn't want to see all the church folk staring at them.

'Where did you meet Jack Cleremont?' Gran asked as we walked home.

'Somewhere near the Park,' I said wildly. 'And he'd

40

seen me ages ago, one Christmas.' My mind was whirling a bit. No wonder Jack talked about trespassers if his father owned the Park!

Gran looked disapproving. 'People say the boy's running wild now his father's gone. I don't think he's a good friend for you, Charlotte.'

'I don't see why,' I said. 'And do they think his father has been murdered or something?'

'Don't be silly!' she snapped. 'He just went off one day. People disappear all the time for various reasons. He must have a lot of money worries, keeping up Cleremont. You would do far better to find friends with stable backgrounds, Charlotte.'

She wouldn't say any more but of course her bossiness made me think Jack would be just the friend I wanted now I hadn't got Cass.

I couldn't ask any more because Freddy Farthingdale came for lunch, which was rabbit pie and Gran's rhubarb crumble. Cass would have hated eating rabbit but I was hungry. I was a bit put off, though, when Freddy said it was one of his rabbits. 'I didn't give it a name,' he said, as if that helped.

Lunch seemed to go on for ages and I grumbled as Gran made me help her clear up. 'Why can't Freddy help?' I asked.

'He needs a rest after his meal,' she said. 'And he's a man.'

Granite Gran had obviously never heard of sexual equality!

Then he needed a cup of tea and the afternoon was half over by the time Gran and Freddy went off for their walk along a footpath trail. More time was wasted as they tried to get me to come too but I said I'd got a holiday book to read for school. That was true, but I wasn't going to read it!

As soon as they'd safely marched off with their backpacks and water-bottles, I ran and changed into my new shorts (we'd each had new ones that summer but mine already looked a bit scruffy while my tidy sister's were pristine). I thought shorts would be best in case I swam to the island. I took biscuits for the white dog and some money to buy myself an ice-cream at the village shop, open on Sundays for the tourists. Gran told me to be sure not to be late for supper at seven because Dad and Cass would be back by then.

There was a coach turning into the gates of Cleremont Park and quite a few people parking their cars on the grass verge just where I could get over the wall. Of course, I'd forgotten about Cleremont Park being open to visitors on Sunday. There was no way I could climb over the wall without anyone seeing me. Luckily, I'd not yet bought the ice-cream so I counted out the money. I'd just enough to pay the entrance to the Park. Now I'd met Jack, I was curious about the place. Also, there was a chance I might meet him again.

I went up the drive and into the house with a group of Wrinklies or perhaps Crumblies, because some of them could hardly walk.

I paid my money to a man at the door who looked at me sharply. 'You're on your own?'

He had a booming, military kind of voice and a thin mouth. I waved at the Crumblies. 'My gran . . . ' I muttered and escaped with my ticket, a free plan of the house and a notice about an Edwardian Weekend.

I glanced at it. **The Red Drawing Room, the Morning Room** (I wondered if there was an afternoon room but I didn't find it), **the Study**, **the Dining Room**, **the Gallery** . . . And masses more besides. How could one family use all those rooms? I began to see Gran's point of view about titles and houses.

Fancy Jack of the holey jeans living here! You could have put all the ground floor of Gran's cottage in the hall and still have some spare room. There were oil paintings, mostly portraits, everywhere.

The man was still looking at me so I dived into the Crumblies, who were listening to the Guide and I recognised Jack's mother.

I trailed after them. I felt a bit cross with Jack, not telling me right off that he lived in this huge house, where parts of the rooms were roped off, to stop people spoiling the valuable furniture, I supposed. Then I heard Jack's mother answer a Crumbly's question and say, 'No – we live in a flat in the East wing. We haven't enough staff to occupy the whole house. A hundred years ago, there were thirteen indoor servants, from kitchen-maids to the butler and twelve outdoor servants – gardeners, grooms and so on. Now we have two ladies from the

43

village to do the housework and one gardener. I do quite a bit of polishing myself.'

'Is there any news of your husband, Lady Cleremont?' one tactless Crumbly asked. 'I didn't think you'd be showing us round yourself, after what I read in the newspaper.'

Jack's mother gave a false sort of smile and her hand, holding notes about the house, shook slightly. 'It's all been exaggerated by the Press,' she said, her voice rather jerky. 'He has only been missing a little while and I am quite sure we shall hear from him at any moment.'

The Crumblies made sympathetic murmurs but I bet they loved being in on something they'd read in the paper. I felt very sorry for Jack and his mother.

I don't think anyone of my age is into old furniture and stuff like that so my mind drifted a bit but when Jack's mother talked about the portraits, I did notice that many of them had died in wars or accidents and she said none in the last century had lived to an old age.

Then we were standing in front of a portrait of a very beautiful woman, dressed in white. She had fair hair, piled on top of her head, looking almost too heavy for her long, slim neck. Her expression was sad and her blue eyes seemed to stare straight at me as if asking for help. I'd seen this expression before, when I looked into the eyes of a gorilla in the zoo, pressed up to the bars of its cage, its brown eyes pleading for freedom.

'Lady Sophia Cleremont, painted just before her tragic death in the lake,' Jack's mother was saying.

'Would that be what they call the Silent Pool?' someone asked.

'Yes. Nobody really knows what happened but of course she may have slipped. I doubt that she could swim. Some say her husband, Sir Thomas, was a bully and a tyrant and she was running away when she fell into the lake. She left behind twin sons, aged nine. We see them in the next portrait, painted with their parents.'

The boys were identical, with gingery fair hair and big blue eyes. But their father, standing with Sophia, was dark and scary-looking and glared down at his wife and children. The Crumblies were oohing and aahing at the sight of the boys and muttering about how sad it was.

Jack's mother pointed to the dark man. 'Their father, Thomas Cleremont, was killed in a hunting accident at the beginning of the Great War.'

She walked to the next big portrait. It was a shock to see the grown-up twins standing by the bridge, leading to the island. 'And here we have the twins as young men painted just before the Great War, perhaps about to leave flowers by their mother's tomb, the mausoleum on the island. James,' she pointed. 'And John. You can tell them apart if you look carefully because James had a big mole or birthmark just above his left eye and John had one on his right. And James, as the elder brother, is wearing a signet ring with the family crest of two herons, with their necks entwined.' She pointed to James's left hand, resting on the bridge. So they were mirror twins, just like us.

45

I noticed that John's lips were pressed together in almost a sneer and his fingers were gripping James's shoulder in what must have been a painful hold.

'James was the elder by ten minutes so he would have inherited Cleremont when his father died. But sadly, he disappeared soon after this painting was finished, at the age of twenty. A gypsy had been seen in the grounds, and James's twin, John, said James had once found him poaching and had threatened to tell the Police if it happened again.'

The Crumblies were all listening avidly and a younger, fat man was scribbling down notes as she talked. 'After James disappeared, a broken window was found in the study where old swords and fencing foils were displayed on the wall. A jewelled dagger had been stolen, also an emerald ring left to James by his mother, intended for his bride. The Police arrested the gypsy but he was later released, for lack of evidence for the theft and also, because James's body was never found.' Her voice dipped and became husky. Then she blew her nose. I thought it was mean to make her do the guiding when she was worried sick about her husband.

The fat man pushed forward. 'Is it true that the gypsy's wife laid a curse on the family and said they would all die violently unless the dagger was found and the true murderer convicted?'

Lady Cleremont frowned. 'It's just a story,' she said shortly.

Someone asked about John.

46

'He married but he was killed fighting in World War I – the Great War. If you visit the ante-room you will see John's uniform and medals and a war diary only recently discovered by my husband . . . ' Her voice faltered. 'John died a hero, saving the life of a soldier who was injured, running out in the face of German gunfire.'

I kept hoping to see Jack as I followed the party down to the huge kitchen with its vast scrubbed wooden table, big black range and masses of copper pans in rows on the shelves.

I was thinking of escaping, to look somewhere upstairs for Jack, when I saw a girl outlined by a beam of sunshine coming through the top of the basement window. She wore a white cap, a dress to her ankles and long apron. She was holding a letter to the light and her lips moved as if she found it difficult to read the words.

I turned back to hear what Jack's mother was saying and when I looked again, the girl had gone. She must be someone dressed up for the part as an old-fashioned maid. We'd done a Victorian Day when we were younger and of course I was made to stand in the corner because I couldn't say my seven times table (can anyone?). Cass loved it, wearing a pinafore and bowling a hoop round the playground.

The Crumblies were examining various ancient bowls, spoons and pots and suddenly I was tired of the house and wanted to find Jack. I guessed it was the dagger he'd been looking for and I was sure I could help

47

him find it, even if it only gave him hope that his father would then come back.

I saw a wooden staircase, not at all like the grand marble one that twisted in a graceful curve from the hall. There should be some kind of back way out. I ran up the stairs and tried a door on the landing which I thought must be the ground floor but it was locked. There was nothing for it but to go on up. The door was unlocked on this landing and I came out on a long corridor with doors on either side. There was someone crying quite nearby.

I ran to the door where I'd heard the voice and opened it. Immediately the crying stopped.

There was a four-poster bed, an uncomfortable-looking sofa and chairs, all behind a red rope to keep the visitors out. I jumped over the rope and went round the room, even peering into the bed's silken draperies. Nobody was there. The sound must have come from another room. I tried to make myself believe that someone was listening to a soap on TV.

The long window looked out into the gardens at the back of the house. I saw a man or boy – it was too far away to see which – running towards the trees surrounding the Silent Pool. There was a gleam as if he carried something shiny. In an instant, he'd disappeared into the trees at the side of the Pool.

Perhaps it was Jack?

I ran back down the wooden staircase and found the kitchen empty. A door was open from the scullery. I ran up some steps, through a yard and then I was outside and running over the lawns towards the Pool.

At last I came to the trees and then I saw there was a path going to the left, which would bring me to the back of the island.

Suddenly there was a rumble and a man came round the other side of the lake, on a sit-down mower. 'You can't go there!' he yelled but I went, although he was moving towards me.

There was a chain across the path and a notice saying PRIVATE but I jumped over the chain and ran along the path, the man's shouts still following me.

It was very hot and I was out of breath. I slowed down and then I was suddenly enclosed in an ear-numbing silence, as if the world had stopped. The white dog slid out of the undergrowth, wagging his tail and staring at me. I held out the biscuits from my pocket and called him but he took no notice.

I ran after him and called as he stood by the bridge. As he began to cross it I jumped in, glad of the cold water against my hot skin and not caring if my clothes got wet because I had to follow him.

I heard barking and growling ahead as I ran down the path and saw Jack, crimson faced, digging a hole in the ground. His dogs were growling softly at the white dog, who stood just behind Jack, snarling and showing his teeth.

'Look out,' I yelled. 'The dog's going to bite you!'

He looked up, startled, and said, 'My dogs don't bite

49

– what are you talking about?' He stepped back, melting into the white dog who reappeared by the mausoleum, a few paces away and began to howl, just like a wolf.

My mind whirled and I stood there, dripping, feeling silly. I knew now that the white dog wasn't real and I guessed he was the ghost of Wolf, the Husky dog, but how could I explain it to Jack? Nobody but Cass would understand.

'Why are you digging?' I asked. I moved nearer and saw a small headstone, the stone I'd sat on the other day, embedded in the ground above Jack's hole. WOLF – *Beloved friend of James Cleremont b. 1907 d. 1913.* 'That's Wolf's grave. You can't dig him up!' No wonder poor ghost-Wolf was upset. He was still whining now, by the mausoleum and I held out my hand and called him softly but he didn't look at me.

Jack stared. 'Are you nuts or what? Anyone would think you'd seen Wolf's ghost!'

'I think I know what you're looking for. I've been touring your house. You might have said you lived in such a grand place.' I felt cross with him now.

'I don't like show-offs. Besides, we'll be selling if my uncle has his way,' he said gloomily, and went on digging.

I wanted to stop him and leave Wolf's bones in peace. 'Why do you think the dagger's in that poor dog's grave?'

'I've already searched the attics, the cellars and cupboards and it's taken me ages. I just thought it might have got buried here.'

'I've been going round the house and I heard about the gypsy's curse.'

'Not all of it, I bet. My mum seems to think it's all a load of rubbish.' He threw a spadeful of earth on the increasing mound beside him. 'After my great-great whatever uncle, James, disappeared, Wolf was found dead on the island by a gardener's boy. James's twin brother, John, said the dog must have been stabbed by the gypsy who'd been seen in the grounds. I suppose Wolf was defending his master.'

Ghost-Wolf was sitting in the shade of the mausoleum, panting and staring at me with those penetrating light blue eyes. I wanted to cry, thinking of his loyalty. 'But if James died on the island, why didn't they find his body? Your mother just said he disappeared.'

'I think the Police searched and they even sent a diver in – wearing one of those old-fashioned diving suits – I've seen an old photo – but the Pool is very deep and they weren't very thorough in those days. Besides, they had caught the gypsy and tried to make him confess to the murder and to where he'd hidden the body and the ring and dagger. But he always denied it and said our family had done a great wrong. That was when his wife cursed us Cleremonts. And that's why I think my father's disappeared. And if the curse can't be stopped, I'll probably die violently too.'

He stopped digging again, wiping the tears and dirt off his face.

'So why do you think the dagger is in the grave?'

51

'I discovered an old newspaper account stuck in a family album,' Jack said. 'The gardener's boy buried Wolf, I guess – I suppose quickly because it was hot, like now. The dog's body was found a few days after James disappeared. The boy's father could have been a friend of the gypsy's and keen to do a cover-up job – telling his son to bury the dagger so fingerprints weren't found.'

'Wouldn't the murderer just chuck the dagger in the lake?' Jack glowered at me for spoiling his idea. 'Anyway, it all happened ages and ages ago. I don't think they'd found out how to look at fingerprints then, had they?' I wanted to stop poor Wolf looking so upset. I was getting used to the idea of a ghost-dog and thought of him as mine, as I seemed to be the only person who could see him, except for the spaniels. I guess they sort of sensed him.

'You really are a know-all!' Jack said angrily and went back to his digging, his bare back glistening with sweat. 'I found this spade all rusty, in the shed. I bet it was the very same spade.'

Poor Wolf was now whining gently at the bottom of the steps leading to the door of the mausoleum. It was shady there, so I could only see a faint white shape. The spaniels sat facing him, grumbling gently but wagging their tails as well, as if they were totally puzzled.

Jack stopped digging. He was staring down into the hole.

'Nothing,' he said sadly. 'Nothing but bones.'

I went to look, feeling sick. There was a dog's

skeleton, partly covered by the dust of the digging and the dirt of years. I turned away and looked for the ghost-Wolf but he had vanished and the spaniels now crowded into the shade where he had been.

Jack looked as sick as me as he gingerly moved the bones and skull with the end of the spade. 'Just in case,' he said.

'Leave him in peace,' I said.

He stopped. 'Yes. Nasty to dig him up anyway but I was desperate.' He slumped down by the hole, his dirty hands over his face.

I felt sorry for him. 'What's the matter? We can look somewhere else.'

'I'll never find it and Dad's never coming back and I hate my Uncle Thomas,' he said in a muffled voice. 'Anyway it's a crap idea, that finding the dagger would help. It's only a stupid legend. I don't suppose there was a gypsy's curse at all.'

I picked up the spade and began to fill in the grave. I thought I would do some detective work. 'What actually happened before your dad went? I mean, did he have any mysterious phone calls – or could he have been blackmailed? Or was he ill?'

Cass and I loved any detective plays on TV; Mum let us watch but Dad disapproved and thought we ought not to be so interested in crime.

He moved to sit in the shade with the dogs. 'I don't want to talk about it.'

It was my turn to wipe sweat off my face. 'I feel the

same about my mum going, I mean, not wanting to talk about it. But it might help if we worked out the details. I mean, the Police could have missed something.'

He looked up defiantly. 'OK! He was worried sick about money and how we could keep this place. We've been trying to get a preservation society to give us a grant – to help us with repairs and so on but no luck yet. And I think there was some kind of row with my uncle. I saw Uncle Thomas with his arm round Mum if you really want to know, by the lake here. Dad and I' – he choked a bit on the words – 'were going fishing. When Dad saw them he just walked away and I followed. He went off that night in his car. It was found abandoned in the Scottish Highlands. They think he might have climbed somewhere and had a fall. Climbing used to be one of his hobbies. They've even had a helicopter out to look but no luck. If he's alive, he'd be running out of the money he took with him and he'd left his cheque book and credit cards at home.'

I felt really sorry for Jack because I knew how he felt about his mum and uncle. My mother used to come back from her art classes all flushed and happy and talking about what a wonderful teacher Zak was. Then there were telephone calls – someone ringing off if I answered. Then that weekend…no, I couldn't think about it.

'Did he leave a note or anything?' I asked after a gloomy silence.

'No. I told Mum it was her fault but she said Uncle

Thomas was just trying to cheer her up because of all the money problems and Dad was depressed. Uncle Thomas came just for a visit but stayed on and on. Everyone thought Dad would come back any moment and Mum wouldn't leave the telephone for days in case he rang up.'

I was streaming with sweat and dying of thirst. I smoothed over the grave and went to sit by Jack. 'Got anything to drink?'

He brought a dented can of Coke out of his pocket and we shared the warm drink, gulp by gulp.

'Perhaps your dad's pretending to be someone else,' I said. 'Starting a new life.'

Jack was indignant. 'He's not a coward! I think he's dead. He's had an accident or topped himself and nobody's found the body.'

I thought I'd better talk about something else. 'Just now, I saw someone from the house – running towards the island. It looked as if he was carrying something shiny.'

'Probably it was Carl again – he's helping his dad today.'

I tried to think how to cheer him up. 'Let's have a swim to cool us off.'

'OK. Mum won't see as she's taking people round. She hates me swimming here. I suppose she thinks I could disappear or something.'

We kicked off our trainers. He jumped in, followed by his dogs and I did a shallow dive off the rotting landing-stage in front of the mausoleum. I beat him to the middle of the pool where he turned on his back and floated.

I trod water and looked back at the island. It was then I saw the couple clinging together on the island in front of the mausoleum – kissing. Then I heard Wolf barking and a man came charging towards them from the direction of the bridge, waving something. It was too far off to see what.

The girl jumped back and the two men began to fight and then ... I knew what was going to happen but all the same I swam back fast to the island. Jack was still floating on his back but the dogs followed me, tired of circling round him.

I heard terrible screams but the men vanished as I landed and looked for my trainers, hampered by the dogs who were shaking themselves all over me.

'What's up?' Jack called from the lake but I took no notice.

Laces still flapping, I ran down the path and saw the girl going over the bridge again. I plunged into the water by the bridge and reached the other side. The girl had disappeared but her hat lay on the ground, as it had before. Something forced me to pick up the hat, put it on my head and then I was full of fear and running, running, crying, towards the wall round the Park. Why was I wearing this bunchy dress that was nearly at my ankles and the stiff black shoes that hurt my feet? But I hadn't time to think of that, I had to get away!

There was a door in the wall I hadn't seen before and I ran through it, onto a dusty lane. My legs took me to the left, in the opposite direction to Elder Cottage, up a hill. A horse and cart turned out of a gate and nearly ran me down, mud spattering on my white dress. The driver shouted something at me but I ran through the gate, still crying and with a dreadful feeling of shock and loss. I told myself I'd been a coward, not to stay. But they were fighting because of me so I had to go.

I was in a sort of Common dotted with gypsy caravans. Lurcher dogs came running but they knew me and didn't bark. I ran home, up the steps and into the semi-darkness of the caravan I knew so well. My father was out, probably shooting rabbits for the pot and my mother, Kezra, was out selling lace and her herbal remedies. I longed to have her comforting arms round me.

For a moment, I sank down on my bed, my face in the rainbow-coloured quilt. He'd told me to run from the fight but now I wish I'd stayed to help him. I hoped so hard that he would run from that evil man and come here for me.

I felt under the bed for the box covered with roses James had given me and undid the lock with the little key I kept round my neck. There was the red rose he had given me, picked from the gardens. It was faded and dead. I pressed the secret spring at the bottom and took out his letters, the wonderful notes and letters he had written me that took so long for me to read. Thanks to my previous position, as kitchen-maid to the Schoolmaster's wife, I'd learnt to read a little and had been given a reference to the Housekeeper at Cleremont.

I sat there, crying still, his letters in my hands, the letters he'd written from Oxford, planning our escape from Cleremont, from his terrible father and jealous brother. I'd kept away from John as much as I could but what James had, John always wanted.

I heard the dogs bark, pushed the letters back and went to the doorway.

Mother was there. 'I knew you were in danger,' she said. 'There's death in the air.'

I rushed into her arms, sobbing.

Then I must have fainted.

'You all right, then?' A girl with a mane of black hair and dragon tattoos on her arms was bending over me. A chain joined the rings in her nose to one ear.

I looked round. The hoop-shapes of the old gypsy caravans were gone. There were modern motor caravans all round, washing strung between them, and two boys on an old motor-bike zoomed past, yelling something at me.

'Where am I?'

'On the Common. We're the travellers nobody wants!' She laughed, and I stared fascinated at the gold stud in her tongue. Dad's so old-fashioned he won't even let us have our ears pierced. 'Heat got you, I expect,' she said. 'Want a drink?'

I'd no idea how long I'd lain here. I looked at my waterproof watch. It was six-thirty. Gran would go ballistic if I didn't get back. 'Thanks, but I'm fine.'

'Take care,' she said and for a moment her voice reminded me of someone else. I felt as if I'd been in some sort of weird dream of the past but already it was fading.

I aimed for the gate, beyond the wreck of a burnt-out car and a pile of rubbish. When I turned round, she was staring after me. She waved a muscular brown arm.

Maybe I'd had concussion or something? Had I really seen men fighting on the island? Jack must have wondered why I ran off.

But Dad would be coming back now with Cass and I had to get back.

I stooped to do up my trainers and when I looked up, I saw the same old woman who had given me a warning before. She was sitting in the middle of the road with her basket, seeming unaware of the car driving towards her.

I ran and hoiked her up under the armpits. She smelled of lavender and fusty old age. Why was she so light that I couldn't feel her weight? I pulled her into the side of the road while the car just tooted at us and drove on.

'You might have got run over!' I said but she just smiled and pointed at something black, lying in the ditch.

Chapter 8

CASS

I knew as we drew up by Gran's cottage that Charlie wasn't there.

Gran looked grim when we came in. 'Charlie still isn't back and she promised to be in for supper. It's very thoughtless of her. After all, I am responsible for her and she's not said where she's gone. I came back from my walk to find the place empty. And the cat's not back either. She always sleeps on the bed on hot days and goes out at night.'

'That girl needs a good talking-to,' Dad said as we went into the kitchen where supper was laid. 'We certainly won't wait for her.'

Gran's onion pie was good but I couldn't eat a lot because I was so worried. Gran was making a big effort, asking me about the day at the seaside and the baby (she didn't mention Zak).

'I took some photos with my Instamatic,' I said.

'It will be nice to see them,' Gran said. Dad was looking at his watch.

'We could go and look for Charlie,' I said.

'Where?' Dad asked but I could tell he was just a little anxious. All that 'stranger-danger' stuff had got to him too.

At that moment, the front door banged – Gran never

locked it – and Charlie came charging in carrying Flora in her arms like a baby. Blood dripped from one paw. Gran's face went white.

'She looked dead,' Charlie gasped. 'She was in the ditch, surrounded by nettles.' She scratched the nettle-blisters on her arms as she talked. 'She must've been hit by a car and crawled there. She didn't seem to be breathing. I didn't know what to do. I didn't want to leave her to get help so I stroked her gently. Then – she was breathing again and making little sounds so I brought her back.'

Gran took Flora from Charlie. 'Thank you, Charlotte,' she said and I could see tears in her eyes.

I wonder if she knew Charlie's secret? We never talked about it but sometimes I envied her and wondered if the healing magic came only to her because she was left-handed, unlike me?

Gran, her face crumpled with distress, put Flora on a clean towel and felt all over her carefully. 'She's not broken anything.' Gran fetched one of her herbal things and dribbled a little into the side of Flora's mouth. We crowded round and all of us, even Dad, smiled when Flora gave another small protesting meow.

Dad insisted on ringing the vet although I was sure Flora would be all right now. As it was Sunday, the on-call vet said he'd open up the surgery for us.

Charlie and I had Flora lying across our laps at the back of the car and smiled at each other when she gave a very faint purr. It was like the old times, doing something together, but when I whispered to Charlie,

61

'What happened? Your clothes are all wet? And I knew you were scared, earlier,' she just said I wouldn't believe her story, which drove me mad with curiosity.

The vet examined the cat carefully and said the car must have knocked Flora's head and caught her paw but it wasn't broken. He said the cat was dehydrated because she could have lain by the road for some time, so he gave her an injection. Flora meowed hard and tried to scratch him.

He smiled. 'Seems as if she's getting better. Wasn't it lucky you found her?'

'My grand-daughter found her,' Gran said proudly and put her arm round Charlie, who still looked as if she might keel over too. I was glad about Gran because she'd been a bit sharp with Charlie before.

When we got home, Flora drank a whole saucer of milk but Charlie hardly ate any supper. Gran gave her a cup of warm herbal tea.

'What's in it?' she asked, sipping cautiously.

'Hops, lettuce, passiflora . . . It should help you relax. And my own honey.'

'Thanks, Gran,' Charlie said dreamily, as if from another planet.

Dad obviously forgot any lectures he was going to give my sister and suggested she went to bed really early and she actually did – Charlie, who never seems to need much sleep and hates going to bed! Flora slipped up after her and curled up at her feet.

I left them to it and went outside with Dad to sit in

Gran's ancient deckchairs. Swallows were swooping gracefully in the evening sky and a few of Gran's bees were buzzing in the lavender bush nearby.

Dad saw me flinch as one flew near. 'Just keep still and they won't sting you out here but I shouldn't go too near the hive when they're active,' he said. 'Of course, I'm used to them. Mum's always kept bees.'

I could see Gran at the bottom of the garden, standing near the beehive. Her lips were moving. 'Is she all right?' I asked Dad.

He laughed. 'Yes! She's telling the bees all the family news. It's an old tradition.'

It seemed weird to me. 'So what happens then? Are they expected to sting her enemies?'

'No – it's just a country habit. I expect she sorts out her thoughts that way. She told me it helped a lot when my father was ill and she had so much to do with running the shop on her own – and looking after me. She gets upset, you know, but won't show it. Rather like me.'

'You got teased at school?'

He sighed. 'A bit. The children found that I had gypsy blood and when I was pretty young we lived with Gran in a gypsy caravan – called a "vardo". I was called Gypo for a while and other worse names.' He sipped at his glass of Gran's elderberry wine. 'Anyway, I learned to put on a bit of armour-plating and look as if I didn't care. After a bit, I didn't care and they stopped.' He sighed and spoke almost to himself, 'But some of the armour-plating stayed on.'

63

I'd never heard him talk so much and I began to see how different he and Mum were – Mum who shouted when she felt angry, hugged us all the time and got excited so easily.

For the first time, I realised how hurt he must have been when Mum went, even if it was right for her.

Charlie says she'll never get married but I want to, one day. But it seems much more difficult than finding a dishy boy and falling in love.

The next morning, Charlie was still asleep when I got up. As usual, she'd thrown her shorts on the floor so I picked them up. A damp, scrunched up paper fell out, half messed up with crushed biscuits. I smoothed out the papers and saw a kind of room plan and also a notice with Clere ... t .ark on top. I supposed it was Cleremont Park. The printing had run on the rest of the paper but I just made out that it was advertising an Edwardian Weekend next weekend. So Charlie had been over the big house and hadn't told anyone, specially not me.

Flora uncurled and came downstairs with me, rubbing against my legs. At least she was friendly.

Gran smiled and began to fuss over Flora, talking to her and giving her a generous bowl of cat food. 'She looks fine now, doesn't she?' she said. 'I named her after my mother, you know.'

'Dad's been telling me he lived with you in his gran's caravan for a while.'

Gran stroked Flora's sleek fur while the cat ate her

food as if yesterday's accident hadn't happened. 'Yes. Her mother, Rose, was completely Romany. She worked for the Cleremonts as a kitchen-maid. But she had Flora – my mother – when she was only seventeen and sadly, died. Flora's grandmother, Kezra, brought her up. Your father is named after Kezra's husband, Reuben, Ben, for short.'

I was getting confused. 'So who did Flora marry? I mean, who was your father?'

'A son of one of the gardeners at Cleremont, Nathan Farthingdale, uncle to Freddy next door. There's Farthingdales all over the village. My father died of the scarlet fever when I was young. So my mother and I went to live with Granny Kezra in her caravan. When I grew up I married your grandfather, Sam Smith, who owned the village shop. He was much older than me and had been wounded in World War 2 so his health was never good. He died when Ben, your father, was a young boy – only a few months after Great-Granny Kezra. He'd left me enough money to buy this cottage so we moved out of the caravan and came here to run the village shop – with my mother, as the old caravan was falling to bits.'

'So neither you nor Dad had proper fathers.' I supposed we were lucky, having both parents – and now Zak thrown in too as an extra, although Charlie wouldn't see it that way.

'Be thankful you have a father,' Gran said a bit severely and I knew she was thinking of how I stuck up for Mum when she left Dad.

65

Dad came down for breakfast, wearing his business suit, saying he was going to a trade fair in Birmingham and he hoped we'd help Gran. He looked almost surprised when I gave him a hug.

Charlie got up after Dad had gone, looking a bit dazed. She ate some breakfast but didn't talk and Gran suggested we both picked runner beans. 'Something peaceful and useful,' she said. 'Better do it now because it looks as though we might be in for another thunderstorm.'

'So what did happen to you yesterday – before you found the cat?' I asked Charlie as we picked. She'd been so much more friendly yesterday that I was disappointed when she just said, 'Something scared me and I fainted. Then I had a sort of weird dream.'

'Why can't you tell me what happened? I know you went over Cleremont Park, I saw the notice.'

She went red and snapped a bean in half. 'You've been nosing around my things.'

'Only picking up your smelly wet clothes!' I said. 'Anyway, why's it a secret? We used to tell each other things.' Then I wished I hadn't said it. Talk about being a sad loser!

'That was before Mum and Zak. You're on the other side now.'

'I'm not! I've been talking to Dad and I know a bit more now how he feels.'

But she was off, stalking out of the side gate and into the lane.

I sniffed back a few tears, then told myself not to be so

66

soft. I'd follow her. That would show her! I let her have a start then I went through the gate.

I'd guessed she was heading for Cleremont Park again so it was easy to follow her through the village but I kept dodging into doorways, thinking she might turn round. I was halfway down the lane with the walls of Cleremont in sight when an old woman came out of a gateway. She was carrying a woven basket full of clothes pegs and bits of lace. She came right up to me, blocking my way so I couldn't see my sister's bright fuzz of ginger hair, far ahead. 'I can't afford ...' I began because I didn't want to disappoint her but she didn't seem to hear.

'Danger,' she said. 'Take care.'

'I will.' I felt a bit scared. She was obviously going senile or something.

I couldn't see Charlie any more so I began to run down the lane.

Then I saw her, past the closed gates of the Park. She was hurrying along the grass verge by the spiked wall.

There wasn't any cover here so I had to hang back until she was almost out of sight. Then I jogged after her. It was already hot and muggy, although the sun was hidden by yellow-tinged clouds and I felt sweat trickling down my back.

I turned a corner. Charlie had vanished!

She wasn't that far ahead so she must have somehow gone over that high spiked wall. I walked beneath it, looking, and found a place where the spikes had fallen off and the wall itself had crumbled a bit, giving some

67

footholds. *Charlie could easily have gone over here but she was good at climbing. I wasn't.*

A car passed me but otherwise, it was too early for tourists and the lane was empty. I told myself not to be a wimp and began to scrabble up, my heart pounding.

'Don't look down,' I muttered to myself and somehow managed to reach the top. I perched there a moment, looking into the dark depths of a wood and then the sound of an approaching car made me swing my legs over and hang by my hands as I scrabbled for a foothold.

I fell down the last bit and landed in brambles. I scrambled out, getting horribly scratched as the brambles clung to my arms.

There was a kind of fork – a path straight on with just a glimpse of the big house in the distance and one to the right. Which way had she gone?

It was spooky in this wood. Even the birds were silent. Then I saw the pale shape of a wolf, running towards me! I remembered reading wolves don't usually attack unless they are hungry and you shouldn't run away so I stood still. Perhaps it had escaped from a zoo.

It stopped in front of me. Then I saw it was some kind of dog with a beautiful thick cream coat and pale blue eyes. I wasn't scared any more as I like dogs. It wagged its curly tail and trotted down the right-hand path, looking once over its shoulder, as if to check I was following.

The path ended at a lake and the dog ran over a rickety old bridge to a small island. I suddenly saw

68

Charlie's unmistakably tatty trainers, by the edge of the water. She must have swum over, I suppose to avoid the broken part I could see in the middle of the bridge. I suppose the dog was light enough to make it safely.

The water looked deep. Why couldn't I swim properly? I just felt scared and swimming lessons at school, with all that noise and splashing, made me feel worse – I kept remembering the huge wave knocking me over when I was little.

I didn't know what to do. Charlie might very well swim back at any moment and I didn't want her to see me because she'd say I was spying on her. I suppose I was, but I felt I could because she kept leaving me out of things.

I sat down behind a tree trunk, where I could still see the island. I could understand why the lake was called the Silent Pool because the trees round it made it breathlessly quiet and rather sinister.

If only the dog would come back to keep me company. What was Charlie doing, anyway?

I was watching a heron, folded up like a grey umbrella on the bank, when I heard loud barking and then a despairing howl from the island.

A man came charging over the bridge, somehow without falling into the hole and I caught a glimpse of a dead white face, all twisted with pain or anger. Then, as he passed quite close to me I saw his loose white shirt was covered with blood!

He looked dangerous – supposing he saw me? I stood, transfixed, as he went on running between the trees. I had time to see him strip off his shirt by a big tree, stopping a moment and pushing something into a hollow. Then he ran off.

He must have hurt the dog! And what about Charlie? I had to get to her. I ran to the bridge and saw I might be able to hang on to the outside edge over the water. I clutched at the splintering wood rail and felt my way along right at the edge of the bridge. Suddenly the wood gave way under my feet and I was falling through into the water!

As it closed over my head, I fought my way up, thinking only of Charlie in danger. I took a great gulp of air and saw the cream-coloured dog staring at me from the island. I struck out desperately and somehow got to the bank and crawled up.

The dog, apparently unharmed, was just disappearing down a path. So the man hadn't hurt it but what about Charlie? My soaked hair was dripping into my eyes so I didn't see so well but when I got to the end of the path, all I saw was a huge marble tomb, reminding me of those in the old cemetery at home, except it was much bigger.

'Charlie!' I yelled several times. I ran round the tomb. There were steps leading down to a door and I saw the dog, lying nose on paws on the bottom step. He was whining softly.

Then I heard a faint voice coming from inside the tomb. 'Help, please help!' Suddenly I had a terrible feeling of evil and death, so strong that I sank down on the top step, unable to move.

70

Chapter 9

CHARLIE

I was floating on my back in the middle of the Silent Pool, looking at the heavy sky. I'd come to the island, hoping to see Jack again or at least the ghost-dog, Wolf, but I saw nothing and it was so hot I decided to have a swim.

It was so scary, having these glimpses of what I knew must be a ghost-world and wondering what it meant.

A dog howled. I turned over so I could see the island. At this distance all I could see was a pale shape, which could be Wolf. There was a dark figure on the ground by the mausoleum and the white flapping shirt of a man running away towards the bridge.

What was happening? I began to swim back and then I heard Cass calling me, loudly, desperately. How had she got onto the island? She sounded scared. I was angry with her for following me but I had to get to her! I was sure now I was seeing not just a ghost-dog, but ghost-people and one of them was evil.

I swam so fast that I was gasping for breath as I got out on the island. The calling stopped and now the silence was worse. I ran round to the back of the mausoleum and my sister flung herself at me in a hot wet hug.

'You OK? I was so scared,' she said. 'Someone's calling for help in there, in that tomb.' She was stammering with the shock of it. 'We have to get inside.'

'We can't. Jack says it's locked and the key's lost.'

'Jack?'

'Jack Cleremont. He lives at the Park and he's our age. I met him here when you were at Mum's.' The relief of seeing Cass was all right made me angry again. 'You followed me here!' I shouted.

'Why not? Why do you always leave me out now?' She began to cry, tears running down her dirty face.

The tears made me feel guilty. 'You know why I go off,' I snapped. 'And how did you get across when you're so feeble at swimming?'

'There's no need to be horrible,' she shouted. 'I saw a man covered with blood and your trainers by the water. And that lovely white dog howled. I had to see if you were both OK.'

She was flushed and angry now and I didn't know what to say. Then I heard it, the faint cry, 'Help!' from the mausoleum.

We looked at each other and rushed together to push on the door. It didn't budge.

'We have to get help,' Cass said. 'Someone could open it with an axe.'

'But the door's been locked for years and they've lost the key, Jack said. There's only Sophia Cleremont buried here and that was about a hundred years ago. The rest of the family's in a vault in the church.'

'Perhaps it's for the tourists,' Cass suggested wildly. 'There's a hidden tape of someone calling for help.'

I was just going to say that the public weren't allowed here, when we heard a loud voice shouting: 'Come out! You've been seen trespassing on the island.'

'I bet that's the nasty uncle,' I said.

As if on cue, the voice said even more loudly, 'My name is Major Thomas Cleremont and my gardener is fetching a plank to put over the bridge.'

I wondered where Jack was. Or had he told on me? I couldn't believe that.

'Can you go to prison for trespassing?' Cass asked, clutching my arm.

'Of course not.' I wasn't sure.

'What shall we do?' Cass asked.

I thought of possible schemes. If I'd been on my own, I'd have swum the other way, across the lake and escaped while Uncle Thomas and the gardener got across to the island but Cass couldn't do that. We could hide in the shed but they'd find us.

'I think the best thing is if we just go to meet them and say we're friends of Jack's.'

'But I'm not,' Cass said.

'He doesn't know that.'

'Why don't we tell him we heard someone calling for help?' Cass said. 'Probably if two men ran at the door it would open, like in crime films.'

'He'd never believe us. I wouldn't have believed it if I hadn't heard. And I think it's a voice from the past, anyway.'

'What do you mean?'

'Can't explain now. Look, he's probably only seen one of us. I'll go.' Somehow I knew Jack would hate his uncle to get onto the island, his private place, and I had to stop him.

'I don't want to stay here alone. I'll go,' and before I could stop her, Cass had run off, down the path to the bridge.

Then I heard excited barking and Jack shouting and Uncle Thomas shouting back. 'Stop those dogs! What do the Police want, Jack?'

Thunder rumbled and I felt a few drops of rain as I crept along the path and saw Cass, half-hidden by a bush at the edge of the path. She was looking at the grass beyond the bridge where Uncle Thomas was hurrying back towards the house with Jack and his dogs. There was no sign of the gardener or the plank.

Had Jack made up some urgent message to keep his uncle away from the island? Or had the Police come to tell them Sir Harry had been found? For a moment, my mind slipped and I saw a crumpled body, lying at the foot of a dark mountain. He had to be alive, for Jack's sake.

'They've gone,' Cass said. The rain was pounding down now, worse than the other day.

'There's a shed . . . ' I began.

Cass interrupted. 'We must get back. Gran will go ballistic when she finds us both gone.'

'Did you actually swim to the island?' I asked.

'Sort of hung on the bridge, fell in and then did two strokes.'

This time she managed three strokes with me swimming beside her, one hand clutching the back of her shirt and keeping her head up. We put our trainers on and ran through the wood to the wall and helped each other climb the slippery bricks as the rain poured down on us. We slithered down and legged it home.

'The dog and the man...' Cass panted. 'Who...?'

'The dog's called Wolf and he belonged to James Cleremont, who died over ninety years ago,' I said panting. I told her jerkily about the men fighting and the girl running away and what I'd heard of the history of Cleremont Park, including the dagger. I didn't tell her about imagining I was the girl running; it sounded too way-out and strange. She'd go back to being the old Cass pretending she didn't believe in ghosts.

'So that man I saw was a ghost who...' Cass hesitated.

'Might have killed James Cleremont,' I finished.

We'd run out of breath by now and slowed down. We were so wet from swimming that the rain didn't bother us except it was suddenly colder. Cass was shivering – whether from cold or fear I wasn't sure. 'I felt the fear by the tomb,' she muttered. Then she clutched my arm. 'There must be a reason that we've seen them.'

'They're stuck in time, like a video, a kind of endless action re-play,' I said. 'Perhaps they always will be, poor things, unless we can find out what happened to James

Cleremont.' Then I told her about the dagger and the curse on the family, a curse laid by our great-great-great-grandmother, Kezra. (I'd worked that out after talking to Gran.) 'I think I've had a warning from her,' I added. 'An old gypsy woman who carries a basket.'

'Yes,' Cass interrupted. 'I've met her too. It's all so weird and yet...'

We didn't say any more as we jogged into the village. Holidaymakers, glumly dressed in anoraks and plastic hoods, were going into The Cleremont Arms to shelter from the rain. It all seemed so normal. I felt we'd been in another dimension.

'Don't you see – we must be here as sort of detectives,' Cass began as we toiled up the hill to Gran's. 'We can see the ghosts because they want to tell us something.'

'We're involved because of our ancestor, Reuben,' I added. 'To find the real murderer of James Cleremont. And to find the dagger and stop the curse on the family so Jack's dad comes back.'

At that moment we were nearly run down by Gran, riding an ancient cycle full-tilt down the lane. We jumped and Gran braked, skidded and slid into the ditch.

We hauled her out. 'You haven't broken your hip, have you?' Cass asked anxiously.

'Why should I do that?' Gran emerged from her anorak hood, her eyes bright with anger.

'Old ladies always do, don't they?'

'I am very fit and not old,' Gran said but she let Cass

hold her arm and I pushed the bike up the last bit.

We put Gran in a chair by the old range and Cass said she'd put the kettle on. 'Hot tea for shock,' she said.

Gran flung off her anorak so wildly that poor Flora, curled up on Gran's winter vest in front of the fire, sprang up, alarmed. 'You aren't listening to me!' Gran cried. 'I am bruised but that's all. But I cannot look after two girls who persist in disappearing.' Her voice was booming now and she looked like Granite Gran again. I thought it wasn't really fair to Cass, who had disappeared only once.

'You will both have to leave and live with your mother and . . .' She still couldn't say Zak's name. 'For the rest of the holidays!'

Chapter 10

CASS

For the next two days, Gran glued Charlie and me to her side. Now we'd become involved in what Charlie called 'the Cleremont Park mystery', neither of us really wanted to leave Gran's for good, not even me.

We helped in the shop, dug up potatoes, ran errands and even did the washing in Gran's ancient machine which danced about alarmingly and leaked a bit.

The good part was that we were talking to each other – we were the Twins again, even if for a short time. Neither of us went into the dangerous area of Mum, Dad and Zak but we discussed the ghosts – the weird way old Kezra had been warning us both and Jack's desperate need to find the dagger and undo the curse on the Cleremonts. We were both longing and yet scared of going back there. I was still convinced we ought to tell someone about the voice in the mausoleum but Charlie said they'd think we were off our heads. I had a strong feeling that she hadn't told me everything that had happened to her.

On Tuesday night we saw something on our local TV news. There were blurry CCTV photos of a man at Edinburgh airport. The TV reporter said that it was thought the photos might be of the Baronet, Sir Harry

Cleremont, who disappeared four weeks ago.

Gran switched it off at that point. 'That family is unlucky,' was all she said.

'Doing a runner from his problems,' Charlie commented when Gran had gone out of the room.

'It might not have been him,' I said.

'Poor Jack,' we both said together.

'We've got to get out to see him,' Charlie said.

But there just wasn't a chance, with Gran in her present mood. And I wasn't feeling all that well, snuffling with a cold and sore throat.

'She's always getting them,' Charlie said when Gran began to make herb tea and made me sit with my head under a towel, sniffing up steam from some eye-watering herbal concoction of Gran's.

I think Charlie's healing powers were in hiding, maybe because she was thinking of the Cleremonts and how to find the key to the mausoleum. Somehow I could feel danger coming, not to myself but to Charlie.

I didn't feel too great on Wednesday but I got bored indoors. The sky clouded up so I went to get in Gran's washing while she and Charlie were in the shop. Freddy Farthingdale's head came over the hedge. I wondered why he didn't use the gate but I guess he's an eccentric. 'Good morning, Charlotte,' he said.

'Cass,' I corrected him. Then I smiled at him. 'Gran's just been explaining that you're my great-uncle or something?'

'Yes, indeed, Cassandra, and very pleased to be.' He thrust a bunch of carrots over the hedge. 'For your grandmother,' he said, as if he'd brought her a bouquet of roses. 'I grow the best carrots in the area but then, I ought to, seeing that my father, uncle, cousin and grandfather were gardeners at Cleremont Park.'

I took the carrots and looked into his face, which was brown and lined like crazy paving. 'Did they ever hear any funny noises or see anything?' I asked.

His shaggy eyebrows drew together in a frown, so all the lines in his face sagged. 'You mean, ghosts?'

'I've sort of heard the place is haunted,' I said carefully. I'd read the booklet from Gran's shop so I knew about Sophia Cleremont's drowning

'You might say that,' he said. 'Nathan Farthingdale, your great-grandfather, and my father were boys, helping out in the garden when Sir James disappeared. My father was off sick that week but Nathan was the one who buried Sir James's pet dog, Wolf. Killed by Sir James's murderer, they say. There was something – but your gran won't like my telling you. Nathan told my father, who told me, that when he found the dog there was a faint voice coming from the mausoleum where Lady Sophia is buried. Of course he couldn't have heard any such thing. At that time she'd been dead more than ten years. So?' The eyebrows went up like furry question marks.

'Did he believe the gypsy killed Sir James?' I asked.

'I don't think so.' Freddy sniffed the air. 'I've got plum jam on the boil and it's nearly ready. Got to go.'

I brought the clothes in, my mind whirling. Later, I told Charlie what Freddy had said.

'Was the noise someone calling for help? Sophia's ghost or...?'

We stared at one another and I knew we were both thinking the same thing.

I sat down by the range because I felt shivery. When Gran came to get lunch she wouldn't talk about James's disappearance, saying it was all past history and best forgotten. Then she suggested I went to bed and I was glad to go and sip her herb tea with honey in it.

I slept a bit and then heard someone knocking at the back door. Gran and Charlie were in the front, in the shop part. I looked out of the bedroom window and saw a boy with curly black hair. He had to be Jack. 'Hi! Charlie,' he said.

'Hi!' I said hoarsely. I don't know why but I thought he'd tell me more if he thought I was Charlie. 'Was it your father on CCTV?' I asked quickly.

'Mum doesn't think so. He'd never leave us and go abroad.' He stared at me so hard I wondered if he'd guessed which twin I was. 'What were you up to on the island? I heard my uncle shouting so I ran out and guessed you were there. Then I pretended the Police were on the phone for him. He rang the Station and luckily, they did want to talk to him anyway.' He kicked at a stone on the path and I saw the holes in his jeans. 'It's been a horrible week and I can't think where to look for the dagger.'

'We – I think what you need to find is the key to the mausoleum. I think it holds the secret.'

'I can't think where it could be.' He sounded very flat. 'And why did you rush off that other time? Swimming to the island as if a shark had got your toe and then when I got there you'd gone.'

I didn't know what to say. Then I heard Gran's footsteps on the stairs. She must have heard our voices. 'I've got to go. I'm meant to be in bed. Got some sort of bug.'

I told her Jack had called round and she said I shouldn't have got out of bed. Charlie was cross because she'd not talked to him. I didn't say I'd pretended to be her and then I felt guilty, afterwards, but after all, she'd hidden something from me.

Mum rang that night and Charlie talked to her. She came up to our room. 'Zak's away, teaching art at a summer school. She wants us both to go there to keep her company. She suggested tomorrow, Thursday and Friday night. She says she misses us,' Charlie said, sitting on my bed. 'She sounded really sad about it.'

I knew that Charlie really wanted to see Mum so I said, 'Why don't you go? I wouldn't want to give my sore throat to Danny,' I added quickly. I longed to see the baby but I knew it was important for Charlie to see Mum and make it up, somehow. And I knew babies shouldn't meet too many germs.

'What about helping Jack? I wanted to get back to the island.'

'A couple of days won't make much difference. Please

go and cheer Mum up.' I didn't say anything about Danny but I knew once Charlie was alone with him, she'd love him.

At last she agreed to go on the train, just for Friday night and Dad would bring her back on Saturday afternoon, on his way from Birmingham.

So, here I am, planning to get better quickly and go to the Edwardian Weekend at Cleremont Park on Saturday. It's time I found out more about the family – and the ghosts – on my own so I can show off a bit to Charlie, for a change.

Chapter 11

CHARLIE

I did it for Mum, really, because I had been missing her, underneath, even if I'm angry with her, too. And I could see Gran was getting fed up with both of us around all day. But as soon as I waved goodbye to Gran and Cass at the station, I wished I wasn't going. I so much wanted to help Jack find the dagger and to work out why those ghosts were haunting us, and apparently nobody else.

Gran wasn't telling us all she knew about Cleremont Park, I was sure. Apart from not liking the place, what was the secret she kept from us?

Mum was standing by the train barrier with the baby strapped in front of her so I couldn't give her a proper hug even if I'd wanted to. She looked so excited to see me, stretching across to give me a kiss. 'I'm so glad you've come, Charlie.'

She led the way to a car park. 'I've a surprise for you – I've passed my test!' And she put the baby in a special chair at the back of a small old car.

'Dad used to say it wasn't worth your trying to pass.'

She smiled as she started the car. 'He took me out a couple of times and I was scared. But I've had lessons and Zak's very patient...' She stopped, knowing that sounded like a criticism of Dad. 'And now Zak's just bought me this little car. I didn't tell Cass last weekend because I wanted to surprise her.'

'It will.' I sat nervously watching the road but Mum seemed OK, if a bit slow.

Zak's cottage was much more untidy than Gran's, with paintings propped up against the walls and on the walls, masses of books and sagging chairs. I could see it would suit Mum's painterly ways and if I'm honest, it would suit me, too.

Mum plonked the baby on a rug and said she'd get lunch ready. So there I was, all alone with the baby. He was wearing a tiny pair of terry shorts and a miniature tee shirt.

I stared down at him. He stared at me with those big dark eyes, slowly waving his arms and legs as if to try them out. I stuck my tongue out at him. You won't believe it, but he stuck out his tongue back! Then he gave a gummy smile.

'Dan,' I said. 'I'm your sister Charlie.' I put out my hand and touched his and his tiny fingers curled round mine.

Mum came back. 'He likes you,' she said hopefully.

'He can stick his tongue out. Cool,' I said in a laid-back voice. I didn't want her to think I was getting fond of him. 'He looks better now he's not so bald.' I'd thought him the most hideous baby in the world when I saw him last time.

Mum had cooked one of my favourite meals, known at home as Mum's Mush. It's a sort of spag. Bol. with

85

loads of tomatoes and olives. Cass doesn't like olives so she always picked hers out. Mum's cooking was either wonderful or really gross. This was a good day.

Dan – I couldn't keep thinking of him as The Baby – was propped up actually on the table in a kind of cute little seat, watching us eat. Mum said she'd fed him before she met me.

'I've missed you, Charlie,' she said.

I concentrated on my food. 'You didn't have to go.'

'Sometimes marriages just don't work out.' She looked at me sort of pleadingly. 'Your father and I are so different.'

'But Dad's on his own now.'

She smiled. 'Very probably not for long.'

Then Dan's snuffly little noises changed to gentle crying and then to mega cries and Mum whipped him off to change his nappy. Ugh! I expect Cass would go and help but not me!

While Dan slept, Mum took me to the barn and showed me her paintings and Zak's. They were pretty fantastic, I thought, because I like lots of colour and exciting shapes but I wasn't ready to go over the top, so I just said they were OK.

There's a stream running through the bottom of the garden which was bright with weeds and flowers and we took Dan down there, to kick in a patch of grass while we leaned against an old willow. It was peaceful. The water made me think of the Silent Pool and I almost told Mum all about the ghosts because she, of all people, might understand. But that meant telling her how much we'd been out on our own and getting into trouble for it.

I'd have grumbled about Gran to her but it didn't seem fair to Gran, who at least had melted down from Granite Gran to Slightly Prickly Gran. I told Mum a bit about Cleremont Park and Jack's dad going missing, which she'd seen on TV.

'That poor boy. Perhaps you can help him,' she suggested. 'It must be terrible not knowing if his father is alive or dead.'

Dan woke up and kicked some more and I gently tickled the soles of his feet so his tiny toes curled. His nose ran a bit and Mum said he'd had a bit of a cold but he looked fine to me.

The crying started that evening, while Mum and I were watching a soap we liked and which Dad said was total rubbish. Mum went upstairs, muttering something about Dan having wind but whatever she did, he still cried. She said he felt hot and he was coughing in a funny way as if he couldn't get his breath.

She walked up and down while I rang the doctor for her.

When the doctor came, she said Dan had a chest infection and croup and as the baby was so young, he'd better go to hospital.

I was almost crying and Mum was trying to be calm while we waited for the ambulance. I hadn't wanted to interfere but Mum took the baby into the bathroom and ran out hot water into the bath, because the doctor said steam might help him breathe. I went in and asked if I could hold him. He looked terribly sick and made awful sounds and suddenly I thought he might die. I knew I couldn't always do it but I held him against my shoulder and stroked him with my strongest hand, my left hand, gently, across his head and the ridiculous stick-up dark hair, now wet with sweat and steam. *Dan get better*, I prayed, making myself just think of him and nothing else.

I knew he'd get better even before he stopped gasping. Mum took him from me. 'He's gone to sleep!' she said. 'It must have been the steam.'

'Yes,' I said, feeling the usual enormous tiredness, like I wanted to sleep for ever.

Of course he was checked over in hospital but they said he must be a tough baby and he'd made a quick recovery.

Cass rang up that night and I told her.

'It must have been awful. I'm glad *you* were there,' she said, sounding really upset.

I yawned. 'He's OK, Dan is. Not bad, for a baby. By the way, I'm staying another night. Dad rang. He's spending the weekend on his own at our house – mowing the lawn and doing some gardening as well as picking up more clothes. He'll bring me back Sunday evening.'

Then I went to sleep like falling into a pit.

88

Chapter 12

CASS

I couldn't stop thinking of baby Dan after talking to Charlie.

'He might have died,' I said to Gran again, at breakfast.

'Well, he didn't, so be thankful,' she said. 'I remember the time your father got measles – they didn't have inoculations against it in those days – and it turned to pneumonia. He was only five. The doctor gave him penicillin but it didn't seem to work. Then I washed him down with my herbal infusions and I knew…'

She stopped. 'What, Gran?'

But she wouldn't go on. To my surprise, after making sure I felt better, she said I could go to the Edwardian Weekend at Cleremont. 'I wonder they are having it, under the circumstances,' she said.

Freddy Farthingdale came to the door just as I was going. 'Where's your gran?' he asked, looking red-faced and anxious.

I called her from the shop. 'Your bees, Kezzie,' he said. 'I saw them early when I was having breakfast, swarming on my fence but when I'd finished and went out, they'd flown away.'

I thought Gran was mean to him because she

snapped, 'You should have come straight away! Now I don't know where they've taken the old queen. I've been so busy I haven't been to the hive lately.'

'Did they sort of kidnap the old queen?' I asked, imagining the bees with little black stockings over their heads and writing ransom notes asking for more sugar.

'Don't be silly, dear!' Gran snapped. 'This happens when the hive is overcrowded. A new queen will hatch out in the old hive but I need my swarm and my old queen to put in another hive. Someone else might take the swarm. It's not stealing once the swarm is off the owner's land.'

It seemed much more complicated than keeping rabbits but I could see Gran was worried. 'Everyone knows you keep bees,' Freddy said soothingly. 'Someone will ring up when they see a swarm. I'll go and look for you.'

'And I'll watch out for them. What does a swarm look like?' I asked.

'There are over thirteen thousand bees in it so it's fairly big.' She held her hands apart. 'Shaped like a rugger ball and hanging point down. But I doubt you'll find them!' She turned to look at me. 'Whatever are you wearing?' I ran off before she could say anything else.

I'd put on a denim mini skirt, a clinging black top, wedgy black sandals that I'd persuaded Dad to let me buy when Mum went (she wouldn't have approved of them) and I'd bundled my give-away hair into a peaked cap. I reckon I looked at least fifteen and not a bit like a girl who would trespass onto an island. Jack's nasty

90

Uncle Thomas was bound to be there, I thought, so I needed the disguise.

It wasn't quite so hot now which suited me as I still felt a bit tired and snuffly.

I walked through the open gates with a handful of other people. A few cars were parked outside the big house. I recognised nasty Uncle Thomas at the door even though he was wearing old-fashioned clothes: a stiff collar and a hot-looking suit with sawn-off trousers and thick socks. He looked like the TV pictures of his twin brother Harry, I thought, except Harry had an open sort of face and Uncle Thomas's was tight and closed.

I followed the guide round: I supposed she was Jack's mother, wearing an ankle-length white dress and her fair hair swept up under a big hat decorated with flowers and imitation cherries. As I listened, slightly bored, to her lecture on the furniture and pictures I was trying to think where the key to the mausoleum might be hidden.

When we came to the portraits, I hadn't realised that Sophia Cleremont was so young and beautiful, nor that her husband Thomas looked so threatening. Of course I knew the next bit, about her death in the Silent Pool.

'Don't they say she had a lover?' asked someone.

Jack's mother gave him a frosty look and went on to talk about James's disappearance and the missing dagger and ring. Also, about James and John being 'mirror twins', James having a birthmark above his left eye and John on the right. Just like us.

I followed the tour round the rooms where a few of the drama group were dressed up and doing what I supposed were Edwardian kind of things. One woman sat at her tapestry-work by a fire. It was far too hot so sweat trickled down her face and I almost giggled. A very pretty maid, dressed in a cap and apron, brought in coal for the fire. In the Smoking Room (funny name, I thought – perhaps there was a ban on ciggies anywhere else, like there is now) three men sat drinking and laughing in a very unconvincing way.

We went upstairs to the School Room.

There was Jack, sitting at an old desk pretending to write on a piece of slate. I had to smother another giggle because he was dressed in a white sailor-suit with blue trimmings! He frowned angrily when he saw his mother but she merely smiled at the severe-looking woman who was pointing to a map of the world and said, 'The son of the house and his governess, having a lesson.'

I winked at him but I wasn't sure he recognised me in my disguise.

At that moment Jack's dogs burst into the room, wagging their tails and jumping round the tour group, some of whom laughed while others looked alarmed. 'Please, Jack!' Lady Cleremont tried to carry it off but she was obviously furious.

The governess fixed a kind of smile on her face and began to spin round a big globe, trying to look as if she still had a pupil. Someone sniggered.

Jack passed close to me and whispered, 'You look as stupid as I do. See you by the Pool.'

After Jack and the dogs made a noisy exit, Jack's mother made some joke about her son's dogs not being trained actors.

A fat man in shorts, who kept pushing his way to the front, asked, 'Is it true that your husband has been seen on CCTV, Lady Cleremont? Did you recognise him?'

'He has been seen but it's not certain that it's him,' she said. 'Are you a reporter?'

'No,' the man said but I saw his hand go to his shirt pocket and fiddle with something. I reckoned it could be a tape-recorder and he was a journalist.

I'd worked out that if Sophia Cleremont was the only person buried in the mausoleum, it was likely the key would be tidied away in some desk or cupboard of her husband's after the funeral. But as that was years ago, both desk and key might have gone.

I looked at the plan and found the Study, which we'd missed out. I slipped out quietly the way we'd come and I was halfway down the corridor when I saw the maid who'd brought the coal – I recognised her heart-shaped face and the big brown eyes. Suddenly a door opened and a youngish man rushed out, gathering her into his arms and kissing her.

They didn't seem to notice me at all. Overacting their parts, I thought. Then the young man drew back and smiled at her and I saw the unmistakable red hair and beaky nose of one of the Cleremont twins in the portrait.

93

Then, quite suddenly, both of them vanished so completely I wondered if I'd imagined them. Or were the actors unusually well made up to look the part?

I felt rather shaky as I hurried on and I felt I had to get out into the fresh air. I ran down the stairs and out of the front door, past the next group waiting to tour the house.

Where was Jack? I ran round the side of the house to a big terrace at the back. The lake gleamed invitingly in the distance and I was sure I could see Jack by the water's edge.

I ran down a flight of crumbling stone steps and across the short grass, tottering a bit on my wedgy sandals.

Jack had stripped off his sailor top and was angrily throwing stones at it in the water. 'Hi,' I said, feeling suddenly shy.

'Oh, it's you, Charlie,' he said in a cross voice. 'I don't know why you had to see all that Edwardian crap in the house. I thought you'd been round it once anyway.'

Of course, he hated that I'd seen him dressed up and looking a real wimp. Should I tell him I wasn't Charlie? He began to walk along the path towards the woods and the bridge to the island.

There was a chain over the path and PRIVATE sign. 'You're not supposed to be here,' he said over his shoulder. 'And why are you wearing those stupid clothes?' I hated the angry way he spoke. What had Charlie done?

I'm not as tough as my sister but I wasn't going to be put off so I followed him over the chain along the path until we came out of the trees.

The blood drummed in my ears as I saw the red-haired man again, running from the island over the bridge. His shirt was covered with blood. He ran across our path, into the wood.

Jack shouted something as I ran after the man, determined to find out where he was going. I knew now the ghost couldn't see me so I wasn't so scared.

I saw him strip off his shirt, tearing at the cloth, and bundle it in a hole in a tree trunk. He stopped for a moment, covering his face with his bloody hands and I saw his shoulders shake. Tears were running down his face as he pulled a big rusty key out of his pocket and thrust it on top of the shirt.

Then he was gone.

I walked to the tree and stared at a big hole in the trunk just above my head. Then I heard a loud buzzing.

I looked up. There it was, Gran's swarm hanging from a branch, a living, buzzing mass of thousands of bees!

Jack was behind me. 'So that was why you ran! You saw the swarm. Are they your gran's?'

'Probably.' I was still dazed, coming back from the ghost-world.

'Better tell her, then.'

His dogs began to bark and Uncle Thomas came, walking fast, his face red and looking silly in his hot Edwardian clothes. 'Tell that girl this part of the grounds is private!' he shouted, then he yelled at the dogs, who were jumping up and pawing his legs.

'I'll tell him to mind his own business!' Jack said, running back. 'You stay, Charlie. I'm not having him telling me what friends to choose.'

Bees – perhaps advance troops sensing an intruder – detached themselves from the swarm and zoomed down at me but I forced myself to reach into the hole. The hollow had grown so big over the years that I had practically to hang over the edge and fish about amongst dead leaves. I supposed the shirt would have rotted by now but the key...

A bee buzzed near my hair. I thought of the voice calling, 'Help!' and the murder I was sure had been done so long ago and made myself go on, feeling with both hands.

All the time I heard the angry voice of Uncle Thomas and Jack shouting back and his dogs joining in with excited yelps. I brought out handfuls of rotten wood, leaves and something that could have been mouldy strips of cloth. Sweat dripped down my back and I thought I felt a bee land on my bare leg but I had one last try and felt something solid and metal in my hand.

I looked round. Jack could help me get to the island. I would have to tell him what I had found. But Uncle Thomas was gripping Jack's arm and marching him back to the house.

Then I looked up at that pulsating swarm above me. I had to get back to tell Gran I'd found her bees. For all

I knew, they might very well fly off somewhere else and never be found.

Suddenly I felt exhausted by the heat and by the shock of seeing the murderous ghost. I didn't want to meet Uncle Thomas but there was no way I could get the energy to climb over the wall.

I walked back, at any moment expecting to be shouted at but nothing happened. I cut across the grass to the drive, dodging behind parked cars and a bus and making my way to the main gate.

Were Gran's bees just an excuse for not trying to get to the island? I'd been dead scared and I knew I didn't want to go on my own.

But I had to find out who was calling me to help them get out of the mausoleum.

Chapter 13

CHARLIE

We were having such a lovely morning, Mum and I, both of us painting in the barn, with Dan asleep in a buggy just outside the open door because Mum didn't think the smell of paint and turps would be good for him. He'd slept well and seemed quite cured this morning but I knew she was watching him carefully after the scare we'd had last night.

I was glad to do something peaceful because I always feel a bit tired after...no, I won't admit to myself exactly what happens when I touch someone who's ill and that tingling begins in my left hand.

I've always enjoyed painting at school but we had watercolours and poster paints. I'd never tried oils before. Mum gave me a canvas board, a few paints, some turps and an old shirt to wear. She set up a still life on a wooden table, of big, over-blown, pinky white roses in a copper vase, against a background swathe of velvet the colour of deep sea in summer.

When I began to draw the roses with thin paint, as Mum had shown me, I remembered the roses painted on the red box in the caravan. Already the whole episode seemed like a dream, as if I'd imagined it. Although I'd often felt things telepathically, I'd never been swallowed up by a ghost from the past like that. Yes, now I admitted the word, a ghost. Supposing I'd stayed there, in the past? I felt shivery at the thought.

I forced my mind to shut down on that scene and concentrated on the roses. When I'd finished the drawing, Mum showed me how to mix the paint and I began to put it on, loving the juicy oils. It was much more fun than the boring things we painted at school and I began to hum as I slapped on the paint, really enjoying myself.

Suddenly, a cold wave of fear made my fingers go rigid so I dropped my brush on the floor. Mum must have noticed my face because she asked me what was the matter. 'It's Cass,' I said. 'She's had some kind of scare.'

'Do you want to ring her?' Mum asked. Of course she knows about our 'twin-twinges' but she plays the whole thing down, maybe because she and Dad feel uneasy about anything supernatural.

I'd brought my mobile for once and tried to get Cass on hers but it was switched off, so I rang Gran.

She sounded out of breath and upset. 'I just heard the phone ring as I came in,' she said. 'I've been looking for my swarm' – what did she mean? – 'and I thought you were someone ringing up to say you'd seen them.'

'Do you mean bees?' I asked.

'Of course,' she snapped. 'No, your sister has gone to the Edwardian Weekend at Cleremont. I'll get her to ring when she comes back.' She hesitated. 'How is the baby? Cass told me. Your mother must have been so worried.'

'Dan's fine, Gran.'

Mum looked up, perhaps hoping that Gran would want to talk to her but she rang off saying Freddy was at the door, ready to help her rehouse the new swarm.

I told Mum all this and she nodded. 'Cass is so sensible. I shouldn't worry. An Edwardian Weekend sounds pretty harmless.'

I wasn't convinced. Supposing Cass had got mixed up with those scary ghosts or fallen in the Pool? I told myself not to be silly and went on painting.

When I'd almost finished, Dan woke up with a hungry cry. When Mum went to pick him up she looked at my painting. 'That's really good, Charlie. Impressionist style. And I like the painting on your shirt, too!'

All the same, at supper-time, I rang again. 'She's fine,' Gran said and she sounded quite bubbly, for Gran. 'She's our heroine, saved the day – she found my bees in the Park and we've fetched them back in my skip with Freddy's help. Lady Cleremont was very nice to us even though they were so busy, but that brother-in-law of hers looked most unpleasant. He kept glowering at us. Here's Cass, anyway. She wants to speak to you.'

'Are you OK, Cass?' I asked. 'Your mobile was switched off.'

'Yes, well, it got wet but I'm all right. I can't tell you now.' She lowered her voice. 'I saw . . .'

She didn't need to finish. 'I know,' I said and I saw the man running, his shirt covered in blood.

'I found something . . .' she began and then I heard

100

Gran calling. 'Got to go. She's done a special meal for me as a reward!'

Zak rang then, and I held Dan as Mum said lovey-dovey things to him but I saw her face, all flushed and happy. I remembered she'd not looked happy very often during the last few years.

Dad knew Zak wasn't there, so he actually spoke to Mum when he came to collect me the next day. She was holding Dan at the time. Dad forced a smile. 'The baby looks healthy enough,' he said. I suppose it was a sort of compliment as he's not into babies.

I looked out of the car window as we drove away. Mum was holding up Dan's tiny hand to wave. I waved back.

'What's that smell?' Dad asked.

I'd smuggled my painting into the car in a plastic bag. 'Oil painting,' I said.

'Oh. Doing it with Mum?'

'Yeah.'

'Good.'

I asked him about our house although Number 22 Thornleigh Road seemed a million miles away at the moment. He happily got away from talking about Mum and painting to telling me about all the mowing, hoeing, etc. he'd done plus collecting letters and clothes. The only thing I really missed now was going to the cemetery and cycle rides with The Gang.

He was just saying we'd be back in time for lunch

when fear came back even more strongly, filling me so much I found it hard to breathe. I thought I could hear screaming and then Cass was somewhere dark and terrifying. 'Drive faster, Dad,' I said suddenly and I rang Gran's on my mobile.

'Is Cass all right?'

'She wouldn't go to church – said she was tired – but now she's gone out and I've a nice roast in the oven. So inconsiderate!' Gran was fuming.

I was just going to tell her to ring Cleremont Park and ask for Jack when my battery went dead.

'Something's wrong. How long till we get home?' I asked.

Chapter 14

CASS

I meant to make myself go back to the Park early on Sunday morning while Gran was still asleep but I was so tired from what had happened the day before that I overslept. Gran woke me up saying she was just off to church and I could stay in bed. She'd left breakfast ready for me.

As soon as I heard the front door bang to, I leaped out of bed. I remembered that when Dad collected me, I'd bundled my swimming things into a bag and brought them back to Gran's, in case she took us to the local swimming pool. I found the bag and put on my swimming costume under my jeans. I stuffed my babyish inflatable armbands, which the school wouldn't let me wear, into my rucksack with the key. It looked very rusty and I wondered if it would turn in the lock.

I went down to the kitchen and found a bottle of cooking oil in the larder. I rubbed some on the key with a kitchen towel. Thinking about the rusty lock, I took a packet of butter out of the fridge and put it in my rucksack.

Then I was outside, running down the road as fast as I could. I almost ran into Kezra. 'Danger – I see danger for you,' she muttered.

I ran on. I turned round and she was still walking up

the hill slowly, as if her big basket weighed her down.

Faint hymn-singing came from the church. I had to be back before Gran.

The Park gates were open, ready for the Sunday visitors, but I daren't go that way in case Uncle Thomas saw me.

It was a heavy morning with the sun hidden behind a blanket of grey clouds and as soon as I'd climbed the wall and dropped down into the wood, it was dusk, almost like evening.

My heart hammered and now I wished I'd waited for Charlie or found Jack to help me. I stood still a moment, hearing nothing but my heavy breathing and a faint cawing from the rooks.

Then Wolf came trotting down the path, waving his curled tail. I was so pleased to see him that I followed him back along the track to the Silent Pool. He gave me a sideways look out of his pale blue eyes and ran over the bridge to the island.

There was a mist rising from the water and a smell of autumn bonfires and suddenly I felt cold.

Now Wolf had gone I was so scared I couldn't move. Supposing ghosts could hurt you? That man with the bloodied shirt . . . I felt sick. Then I told myself that I had – literally – the key to the mystery: I wanted to find the truth and help Jack but still I stood there, trembling.

Then I thought I could hear barking. Perhaps I could stop the past repeating itself and at least save Wolf from death. Could you alter the past?

I undressed, put on my armbands and strapped on my backpack, hoping I could keep it dry. I slid into the water and struck out, helped by the armbands.

I crawled up the bank and crept along the path.

The pale marble of the mausoleum gleamed through the mist. I found Wolf, crouched by the door. There was a faint sound from inside and he whined.

'I'm coming to help you,' I said to whoever-it-was inside and went to the door. Wolf just melted away.

I felt sick at the thought of going inside – I hate dark, enclosed places – but I took the key out of my backpack, put it in the lock and tried to turn it. It wouldn't budge. I fiddled with the damp packet of butter, putting some round the end of the key.

As I put it in I heard low voices behind me. I turned, and saw the back view of a girl wearing an ankle-length dress and a straw hat, the girl I'd seen as a maid at Cleremont. A red-haired man was holding her close. He moved slightly and now I could see his face and the birthmark just above his left eye, so it was James Cleremont. The couple kissed and then Wolf was barking and John Cleremont came running, his face twisted with anger and a dagger in his hand!

He yelled at his brother – but I couldn't hear the words – and James shouted back and turned to the girl, pushing her towards the path. She ran, sobbing, tears running down her face.

I stood, transfixed with horror, watching a fight I couldn't prevent. John slashed at James with the dagger, wounding his arm but James fought back, twisting away and then hitting out while Wolf tried to defend his master, growling and biting at John's legs.

Then John turned, still shouting and thrust the dagger into Wolf's side. The dog collapsed to the ground with a howl of pain. James turned and saw Wolf. His face twisted with grief and at that moment, John stabbed him. He screamed and blood spurted out, splashing John's shirt. Then James collapsed to the ground so near me I could see his contorted face.

I was nearly sick. I couldn't think straight. I had to escape from this terrible scene! Suddenly I felt the ghosts were so real that John would stab at me too if I tried to pass him. I tried the key again and the lock turned. The door opened so suddenly I almost fell inside the darkness of the mausoleum.

The horror followed me – John was there, thrusting James's body on top of me. I smelled sweat, blood and felt the sickening weight on me. I screamed but there was nobody to hear me.

Then the door shut me into suffocating darkness.

Chapter 15

CHARLIE

As soon as Dad stopped the car, I leaped out and tore into the cottage. Gran came out of the kitchen, looking upset. 'Cass?' I asked and when she shook her head I ran straight out again, past Dad and down the lane.

I thought I heard the car behind me so I dodged into The Cleremont Arms garden where tourists were sitting out, pretending the sun still shone.

Cautiously, I looked round, sheltered from view by a very large woman. Was that Dad's red Estate car? I waited a moment, then doubled back into the lane.

The old woman we thought could be Kezra seemed to spring out of the ditch, blocking my way. She mumbled something which sounded like a warning which I didn't need.

'Did you see her?' I asked stupidly.

A family looked at me strangely as they passed and the children giggled. Their father put out his hand to point at a field of sheep. His hand went straight through Kezra and she disappeared.

The gates to Cleremont Park were open and I decided to risk it. Climbing up the wall with this amount of people round would attract attention. Had Dad driven inside? I'd risk that too. I made myself walk through the gates and along the drive, shielded by cars driving up to the house. Near the house I ran across the grass to the Pool as fast as I could. I thought I heard someone calling but I didn't look round.

When I drew near the Silent Pool, the air seemed to thicken and the sky darken and I felt really scared.

Suddenly, Wolf came out of the dark trees. He ran ahead over the bridge and stood on the bank, panting. Then he sat, pointed his nose to the sky and howled, the sound nearly drowned by a sudden wind in the fir trees round the pool. Branches began to creak and wind ruffled the water and the crows flew up, cawing loudly.

Then I saw Cass's clothes on the bank. She must have swum across to the island.

I pulled off my trainers and plunged in. As I reached the island I heard the distant sound of dogs barking. Wolf had disappeared again.

Now I was on the island and a man ran along the path towards me, his shirt bloody, tears pouring down his face. My heart almost stopped as he ran straight through me towards the bridge.

The clearing was empty. 'Cass, Cass!' I called desperately. Then I saw Wolf scratching at the door to the mausoleum. I could see the strong muscles in his legs and the way his hair stood up like a ruff round his neck. It seemed impossible that he was a ghost-dog.

But Cass couldn't have got inside without the key, could she? And she'd be scared anyway. She hated enclosed spaces: she didn't even like going in lifts and when we looked into a cave once on holiday she backed out, saying she felt she was going to suffocate.

So she'd never go inside without me. Wolf stopped scratching and looked back at me and then I heard the voice again, saying, 'Help me,' very faintly.

Wolf melted as I went through him. And then I saw that the key was in the lock. I turned the key but it seemed to be stuck.

I went back up the steps and then charged the door with my shoulder. The pain made me reel but the door opened and I fell inside on something soft and warm...

'Cass!' I said, rolling off her.

Then the wind blew the door shut and we were in total darkness, darkness that smelled of death and decay.

Chapter 16

CASS

Something heavy fell on me and I was swimming up, fighting dark waters of fear, and then I heard dogs barking and Charlie was there, her arms round me. 'I'm here. I'll get you out,' she said.

'The door's locked,' I muttered. John had locked me in before he ran to the wood. 'We'll die in here.'

'It was only stuck,' Charlie said, pushing at it but it didn't move. Then we heard barking outside and she was shouting, 'Help!' just like ...

There was a scuffle outside and then the door was open, flooding the place with wonderful light. Jack, Merry and Magic were peering inside. 'What are you doing in there?' he asked. 'Where did you get the key? I noticed a movement on the island so I came over...'

'Move out the way,' Charlie snapped, helping me out. I collapsed on the steps. My legs were so weak.

Jack and the dogs had gone inside. I heard him telling them to sit and then he actually screamed, then swore and shot out again, the dogs behind him. He shut the door violently.

'What is it? Did you see the dagger or anything?' I asked him.

'This is so gross.' And his normally rosy face was

dead white. He was gasping for breath as he gabbled, 'There's a skeleton beside a sort of stone coffin. And there's a dagger...' He couldn't finish.

We stared at him. I knew Charlie was thinking the same as me, that we had to tell Jack about the ghosts. But would he believe us?

Jack sat down on the top step. 'I was coming to tell you – I took John's war diary out of the glass case, to see if it gave any clues about the dagger. The writing was faded and it was hard to read but there's a page which makes me think he killed his brother.'

He was wet from the swim but he fiddled in a back pocket and brought out a small package wrapped in what looked like a freezer-bag and sealed with tape. 'It's only been in the glass case a short time. Dad found it in an old desk just before...' He turned over the pages. 'It took me ages to read and most of it's about the First World War. It's the last entry that matters.'

He read slowly:

November 20th 1917: We are waiting for reinforcements but I doubt they will come. Noise and smell terrible. Rats. Thick mud. Private Brown, standing next to me in the trench, had his head blown off. I have Seen my death tomorrow. I wish I could see my children and wife again but my conscience has plunged me into Hell after James's death, the death of my other half whom I miss sorely. At least now I can pay the price.

111

'At least he was sorry,' Charlie said.

'It must have been awful for him,' I said faintly, feeling the horror of it. 'Killing his twin.'

'What do you think you're doing here?' shouted a voice.

We turned to see Dad and Uncle Thomas, running towards us, looking angry. 'We saw you from the lakeside and my gardener put a plank over the bridge,' Uncle Thomas said.

'You found her!' Dad rushed to hug Cass.

'And they found the dagger. And what must be James Cleremont's skeleton,' Jack said.

Uncle Thomas stared at him as if he didn't understand. 'How did you get into the mausoleum? I thought that key was lost long ago.'

'I found it in a hollow tree,' I said. 'Where the murderer left it.'

'Wasn't there a gypsy?' Uncle Thomas began.

Charlie and I interrupted him, speaking together. 'No! James's twin brother John killed him and we can prove it.'

Chapter 17

CHARLIE

I suppose I'd expected them to believe us and then Jack's father would come marching up the drive, now we'd broken the curse but it didn't happen like that. We went to a flat in a wing of the house, where the Cleremonts lived.

Jack's mother looked really upset. I suppose even though the murder was years ago, any death reminded her of her husband's disappearance.

'The dagger was there, I saw the hilt,' Jack said. 'Right through the ribs of poor James.' He paused, then said, 'Doesn't that mean Dad will come back?'

His mother put her arm across his shoulder. 'That is just a superstition, darling,' she said to him. Then she had a fierce but quiet discussion with Uncle Thomas who wanted to finish the Edwardian Weekend before calling the Police.

Jack wanted to know why he couldn't keep the dagger and then have a funeral for poor James.

'The Police are involved. The skeleton must be properly identified first,' his mother said. 'We can have a funeral later.'

'This discovery should bring the visitors flocking in,' Uncle Thomas said, rubbing his hands. 'Maybe we won't have to sell, after all.'

Jack's mother gave him a cold look. 'Do we want that kind of publicity?' she asked.

I had the feeling that Jack was wrong – that she didn't really like Uncle Thomas very much.

Someone brought us tea, which I hate, but Cass drank hers and looked better.

Dad rang Gran to say Cass was all right but the Police had said we should stay to answer questions.

I thought it was exciting when a Detective Inspector and a Sergeant arrived, just like on TV, but Cass said she wanted to go home. They asked us questions. Cass found it hard to explain why she'd looked into the hollow tree and found the bits of shirt and the key but Dad had told us to tell them everything we knew.

'I was looking for Gran's bees,' Cass said in the end.

The Inspector looked at us. 'It seems a strange story – the way you girls found the skeleton.'

We said nothing. He had no idea how strange it was.

At last the policemen went to the island with Uncle Thomas and Jack's mother, who looked ashen-faced. Jack insisted on going with them.

Dad took us home. Jack's mother must have won about closing the house, because the visitors and actors were coming out of the front door and I recognised the woman who was the governess.

As we walked to where our car was parked, a fat man I'd seen before wobbled up to us. 'I gather the Police are making enquiries about a skeleton found in the grounds?'

'We found it!' I said proudly. 'And it's John Cleremont who killed his brother James about ninety years ago, not our ancestor Reuben the gypsy.'

'Come on, Charlie,' Dad said quickly. 'Nothing's official yet. The Cleremonts won't want us to talk to people.'

'Do you live in the village?' the man was asking but Dad hustled us into the car and drove off.

'I've seen him before, asking questions,' Cass said.

Dad sighed. 'He'll be a journalist.'

When we got back, Gran seemed much more interested in fussing over Cass than listening to the story of our great discovery but Freddy Farthingdale, who 'popped in' as he put it with some of his bolting lettuces, was quite excited. 'What a story!' he said. 'My dad always said his dad knew who the murderer might be. I wonder what happened to that ring.'

I wanted to go and find out more from Jack but Dad told us to leave the Cleremonts alone for the rest of the day and then he got his laptop out to do some work, of all things. Trust him not to get too excited!

The weather had turned, the wind that had blown the mausoleum door shut (but Cass said privately to me she was sure John's ghost did it) grew and fitful spurts of rain came out of a grey sky. Cass said she felt cold and went to sit by the range in the old basket chair with Flora on her lap.

I felt flat. I supposed now Wolf had shown us where his master was lying, I wouldn't see him again. And

115

maybe it was just superstition that Jack's father would return. None of this would mean anything to Jack if his father were found dead on a lonely mountain.

I suppose Gran wanted to distract us from talking about the skeleton so she brought out a pile of old photo albums. Normally we'd have enjoyed giggling at photos of baby Dad kicking on a rug, a skinny Dad in a school photograph, Dad making a sandcastle and so on but today we were too churned up to concentrate. There were even tiny black and white photos of Gran as a baby in her mother's arms. 'That's my mother, Flora,' Gran said. 'As I told you, her mother Rose died when she was born.'

I looked at Gran's mother, at her curly hair and heart-shaped face. 'She looks like Rose,' I said and Gran gave me a sharp look.

I turned a page. 'Who's that?' I peered at the small black and white photograph of an old lady with a small girl on her lap. She even wore a shawl round her shoulders.

'That's Kezra, my great-granny with me – in my best dress, too!' Gran smiled. 'She brought my mother up. She still went on going round the village selling things like clothes pegs until she was quite old.'

Cass and I looked at each other, remembering. We knew now that Kezra had wanted us to clear Reuben's name.

'The Kezra who put the curse on the family,' Cass said.

Gran's face tightened. 'All that superstition!' she snapped.

'She came to help us lift the curse,' Cass murmured but I don't think Gran heard.

116

n's war diary. They've taken John's uniform away – ...e kind of DNA test on an old bloodstain or ...ething and they'll do one on poor James's bones as ...l, to identify him. And I think they're doing tests on ...tiny bits of shirt from the hollow tree. At least it will ...w the same DNA as James, so Reuben couldn't have ...e the murder because Mum says identical twins have ...same DNA.'

...e stopped his full-speed chatter to take a breath. ...n he went on, 'I don't really know about it but it's ...lar cells or something. Maybe the blood's too old, ...gh, and they'll just let the matter drop because ...'s nobody alive to put in prison but I think the war ...might convince them.'

...u ought to read this letter, Cousin Jack,' I said, ...ng it at him.

...usin?' he muttered.

...n he'd read it, he sighed. 'Fancy murdering for ...a girl!'

...ed at Cass and she smiled and blew her nose. ...dn't expect a boy to understand that part of it!

...do you mean, "cousin"?' Jack asked.

...ere in the middle of explaining when I heard ...V go on in the sitting-room. Dad called us in. ...omething about Cleremont here.'

...ught the end of the News, the part where they ...news. A picture of Cleremont Park flashed on ...nother of the island with the dome of the ...showing. A reporter was saying, '...in a

'What's that?' I went over to the dresser and saw a familiar red box covered with roses. The time when I was caught in the past was fading now but I'd seen this box before, in a gypsy caravan. Letters...I picked up the box. It had been locked but not now. I lifted the lid and looked inside.

'It's only trinkets in there,' Gran said. 'I don't know why I kept it. I believe it belonged to Rose, my grandmother.'

'I fetched Gran's bee skip from the attic and brought down that box because it was so pretty,' Cass said.

Gran exclaimed, annoyed at the mess, as I tipped out cheap jewellery, tarnished with age onto her clean kitchen table. There was a necklace made of shells, dust, bits of what could have been dried leaves or flowers, beads, an embroidered purse, a silver bracelet. Then I felt round the bottom of the box. What was real and what had I imagined? My finger touched a tiny button and the bottom came up, like a flap. I looked at the envelopes and the faded ink.

'They aren't ours to read,' Gran said but Cass and I took no notice. We spread them out on the table and in the end, Gran looked at them too.

There were only two: letters from James to Rose, sent when he was at Oxford with John, just before World War 1. The ink had faded and the writing was difficult to read.

The first was short, saying how much he missed her but they would see each other soon.

I read out the second, longer letter, dated May 25th, 1913 and simply headed, St. John's, Oxford.

My dearest Rose,

I miss you so much and think all the time of our meetings on 'our' island. Soon John and I will come down for the summer vacation. I'm so excited to hear you are carrying our child. Will you marry me, my darling, sweet little Rose? I am making plans now for us to run away and marry at Gretna Green in Scotland, away from my terrible father. I have my share of the money our mother left John and me and we can live in a little cottage and be happy. I even have a ring for you that my poor mother left me for my bride, as I am the elder son.

Your father and mine can do nothing when we are safely married and our child is born.

I think John may have guessed about us because he looks at me angrily and avoids me when he can. I've seen him looking at you at home and I believe he is half in love with you himself.

Hide this letter or burn it. If only I owned Cleremont I could do as I liked but I am not even of age yet. My father deserves to die for his cruelty to my mother which drove her to her death – but you know what he is like because all the servants dislike him, too.

But that's enough. This is to send all my love. I have written carefully so you can read it more easily, my beautiful, clever Rose.

I shall love you always, James

We were silent a moment, then Cass l
so sad. They really loved each other. I
then she died having his baby.'

Gran was the first to break the
promised to marry her and he knew a
don't think my family ever forgave the

'Why didn't Rose fetch the Police?
mean – she must have guessed John h
even if she didn't actually see it happen

'Remember – John tried to put the bl
I said. 'And neither the weapon nor th
I suppose that's why the case was
there wasn't enough proof.'

'And who would believe a gyps
worked as a maid at Cleremont?' G
she was protecting her father.'

'I suppose John loved her too a

'And he probably wanted to i
said in a bitter voice. 'Money
very often.'

I was thinking hard. 'If we
and James, then Jack's a sort

At that moment, our sort-c
'Is Cass OK?' he asked str
asked about me, I thought.

Gran asked him to come

He was bursting with
emerald ring under the sk
in his pocket to give t

Joh
som
som
wel
the
sho
dor
the
H
The
simi
thou
there
diary
'Yo
thrust
'Co
Whe
love of
I loo
We cou
'Wha
We w
Gran's T
'There's
He'd c
have loca
and then
mausoleur

mausoleum erected to house the coffin of Lady Sophia Cleremont, who died in 1902. It is thought the skeleton may be of Sophia's twin son, James, who disappeared in 1913. Ironically, Sir Harry Cleremont, Baronet, the present owner, is also missing in the Scottish Highlands...' They showed a photograph of Jack's father. Dad switched the TV off but not in time.

Jack crumpled up on Gran's sofa, his shoulders shaking. 'Why don't you come home?' he said, his voice muffled by a cushion.

Dad went off in the morning. He didn't seem very interested to find he was related to a titled family but then, Gran had brought him up to think owning titles and great houses was wrong. Gran didn't seem excited either and I think we were all sad for Jack, who was still crying when Dad took him home on Sunday night.

'Poor lad. And reporters will be all over the place for a good story,' Gran said.

She was right. Charlie and I went to the village shop to get some things for Gran which included a paper. The village seemed to be full of people and cars and we saw a TV van driving towards Cleremont.

The article wasn't on the front page but further in. There was another picture of Cleremont Park with the headline: *WAS THIS MURDER? DID JAMES CLEREMONT DIE BY HIS MOTHER'S COFFIN?* There was a close-up photograph of the mausoleum on the island. Gran said they must have used special long distance lenses for that. The article got it all wrong (Gran said papers always got things wrong), saying Jack had found the skeleton – no mention of us at all! And it went on a bit about the coincidence of it happening in the middle of an Edwardian Weekend at Cleremont.

Then there was a weird bit at the end saying Thomas Cleremont was at present helping with enquiries about his brother's disappearance.

'Do you think Thomas is another bad Cleremont and he could have killed Harry?' I suggested.

Cass looked into the distance, as if she could see something but she didn't answer. I felt upset because I didn't know what she was thinking about.

We'd run into the shop to show Gran the article but she hadn't time to read it because more and more customers came in, so many that we had to help her. She ran out of copies of the booklet about Cleremont and sold all the postcards as well as lots of her herbs and honey.

She shut the shop for lunch. 'They won't like all this publicity,' was all she said as we ate our cheese sandwiches. Mum rang up, having heard the news, and she seemed sorry for the Cleremonts, too. Her newspaper had said schoolchildren trespassing in the grounds of Cleremont Park had found the skeleton and I squeaked, 'Mum – that was us!'

When we'd finished telling her, she said, 'By the way – will you be too busy with reporters or are you coming for the weekend?'

It was my turn to talk to her at that moment and I

'What's that?' I went over to the dresser and saw a familiar red box covered with roses. The time when I was caught in the past was fading now but I'd seen this box before, in a gypsy caravan. Letters... I picked up the box. It had been locked but not now. I lifted the lid and looked inside.

'It's only trinkets in there,' Gran said. 'I don't know why I kept it. I believe it belonged to Rose, my grandmother.'

'I fetched Gran's bee skip from the attic and brought down that box because it was so pretty,' Cass said.

Gran exclaimed, annoyed at the mess, as I tipped out cheap jewellery, tarnished with age onto her clean kitchen table. There was a necklace made of shells, dust, bits of what could have been dried leaves or flowers, beads, an embroidered purse, a silver bracelet. Then I felt round the bottom of the box. What was real and what had I imagined? My finger touched a tiny button and the bottom came up, like a flap. I looked at the envelopes and the faded ink.

'They aren't ours to read,' Gran said but Cass and I took no notice. We spread them out on the table and in the end, Gran looked at them too.

There were only two: letters from James to Rose, sent when he was at Oxford with John, just before World War 1. The ink had faded and the writing was difficult to read.

The first was short, saying how much he missed her but they would see each other soon.

I read out the second, longer letter, dated May 25th, 1913 and simply headed, St. John's, Oxford.

117

My dearest Rose,

I miss you so much and think all the time of our meetings on 'our' island. Soon John and I will come down for the summer vacation. I'm so excited to hear you are carrying our child. Will you marry me, my darling, sweet little Rose? I am making plans now for us to run away and marry at Gretna Green in Scotland, away from my terrible father. I have my share of the money our mother left John and me and we can live in a little cottage and be happy. I even have a ring for you that my poor mother left me for my bride, as I am the elder son.

Your father and mine can do nothing when we are safely married and our child is born.

I think John may have guessed about us because he looks at me angrily and avoids me when he can. I've seen him looking at you at home and I believe he is half in love with you himself.

Hide this letter or burn it. If only I owned Cleremont I could do as I liked but I am not even of age yet. My father deserves to die for his cruelty to my mother which drove her to her death – but you know what he is like because all the servants dislike him, too.

But that's enough. This is to send all my love. I have written carefully so you can read it more easily, my beautiful, clever Rose.

I shall love you always, James

We were silent a moment, then Cass began to cry. 'It's so sad. They really loved each other. First he dies and then she died having his baby.'

Gran was the first to break the silence. 'James promised to marry her and he knew about the baby. I don't think my family ever forgave the Cleremonts.'

'Why didn't Rose fetch the Police?' Cass asked. 'I mean – she must have guessed John had killed James even if she didn't actually see it happen.'

'Remember – John tried to put the blame on Reuben,' I said. 'And neither the weapon nor the body was found. I suppose that's why the case was dropped, because there wasn't enough proof.'

'And who would believe a gypsy girl, even if she'd worked as a maid at Cleremont?' Gran said. 'They'd say she was protecting her father.'

'I suppose John loved her too and was jealous,' I said.

'And he probably wanted to inherit the Estate,' Gran said in a bitter voice. 'Money means more than love, very often.'

I was thinking hard. 'If we're descended from Rose and James, then Jack's a sort of cousin.'

At that moment, our sort-of-cousin came to the door. 'Is Cass OK?' he asked straight away. He might have asked about me, I thought.

Gran asked him to come in.

He was bursting with news. 'The Police found the emerald ring under the skeleton. I suppose James had it in his pocket to give to Rose. Then I showed them

John's war diary. They've taken John's uniform away – some kind of DNA test on an old bloodstain or something and they'll do one on poor James's bones as well, to identify him. And I think they're doing tests on the tiny bits of shirt from the hollow tree. At least it will show the same DNA as James, so Reuben couldn't have done the murder because Mum says identical twins have the same DNA.'

He stopped his full-speed chatter to take a breath. Then he went on, 'I don't really know about it but it's similar cells or something. Maybe the blood's too old, though, and they'll just let the matter drop because there's nobody alive to put in prison but I think the war diary might convince them.'

'You ought to read this letter, Cousin Jack,' I said, thrusting it at him.

'Cousin?' he muttered.

When he'd read it, he sighed. 'Fancy murdering for love of a girl!'

I looked at Cass and she smiled and blew her nose. We couldn't expect a boy to understand that part of it!

'What do you mean, "cousin"?' Jack asked.

We were in the middle of explaining when I heard Gran's TV go on in the sitting-room. Dad called us in. 'There's something about Cleremont here.'

He'd caught the end of the News, the part where they have local news. A picture of Cleremont Park flashed on and then another of the island with the dome of the mausoleum showing. A reporter was saying, '. . . in a

120

mausoleum erected to house the coffin of Lady Sophia Cleremont, who died in 1902. It is thought the skeleton may be of Sophia's twin son, James, who disappeared in 1913. Ironically, Sir Harry Cleremont, Baronet, the present owner, is also missing in the Scottish Highlands...' They showed a photograph of Jack's father. Dad switched the TV off but not in time.

Jack crumpled up on Gran's sofa, his shoulders shaking. 'Why don't you come home?' he said, his voice muffled by a cushion.

Dad went off in the morning. He didn't seem very interested to find he was related to a titled family but then, Gran had brought him up to think owning titles and great houses was wrong. Gran didn't seem excited either and I think we were all sad for Jack, who was still crying when Dad took him home on Sunday night.

'Poor lad. And reporters will be all over the place for a good story,' Gran said.

She was right. Charlie and I went to the village shop to get some things for Gran which included a paper. The village seemed to be full of people and cars and we saw a TV van driving towards Cleremont.

The article wasn't on the front page but further in. There was another picture of Cleremont Park with the headline: *WAS THIS MURDER? DID JAMES CLEREMONT DIE BY HIS MOTHER'S COFFIN?* There was a close-up photograph of the mausoleum on the island. Gran said they must have used special long distance lenses for that. The article got it all wrong (Gran said papers always got things wrong), saying Jack had found the skeleton – no mention of us at all! And it went on a bit about the coincidence of it happening in the middle of an Edwardian Weekend at Cleremont.

Then there was a weird bit at the end saying Thomas Cleremont was at present helping with enquiries about his brother's disappearance.

'Do you think Thomas is another bad Cleremont and he could have killed Harry?' I suggested.

Cass looked into the distance, as if she could see something but she didn't answer. I felt upset because I didn't know what she was thinking about.

We'd run into the shop to show Gran the article but she hadn't time to read it because more and more customers came in, so many that we had to help her. She ran out of copies of the booklet about Cleremont and sold all the postcards as well as lots of her herbs and honey.

She shut the shop for lunch. 'They won't like all this publicity,' was all she said as we ate our cheese sand-wiches. Mum rang up, having heard the news, and she seemed sorry for the Cleremonts, too. Her newspaper had said schoolchildren trespassing in the grounds of Cleremont Park had found the skeleton and I squeaked, 'Mum – that was us!'

When we'd finished telling her, she said, 'By the way – will you be too busy with reporters or are you coming for the weekend?'

It was my turn to talk to her at that moment and I

hesitated, because I felt neither of us would want to leave the village in case we had news of Jack's father. We had to be there if Jack needed to talk.

Mum must have thought I didn't want to come so she said, 'Never mind, Charlie. Another time,' but she sounded sad and rang off before I could explain.

When Gran popped out to see her new bee colony before reopening the shop, Cass said thoughtfully, 'James and John must have had a horrible life after their mother died. They were only about nine and I bet their father was cruel. Perhaps that brought out John's nasty side?'

Cass was always so ready to see the best in anyone. 'Except James had the same father and he was all right.'

'I get the feeling that John might always have been a bit envious of James,' Cass said quietly. 'Maybe James was bolder and better at things and pretty Rose fell for him, not John, remember.'

Was this what Cass felt about me? No, I thought it couldn't be the same at all. 'I wonder if James and John knew each other's feelings?' I said quickly.

'And did they see ghosts too?' Cass suggested. 'Perhaps James liked the island because he saw his mother there?'

We never finished that discussion because two reporters came to the door asking questions. We were busy telling them the bits without the ghosts – because nobody would believe that – when Gran came storming in and drove them away.

We were watching the local news again, hoping to hear something about ourselves, when the telephone rang. It was Jack.

'I can't talk long. And don't tell anyone but your gran because of the reporters,' he said, jabbering again with excitement. 'My dad's coming back! He'd lost his memory – I suppose through worry and he'd been sleeping rough. Then he went to buy food and bought a newspaper. He saw the article about Cleremont and it brought his memory back so he rang Mum up. We're going to fly to Scotland and fetch him. And Mum's had a row with Uncle Thomas and sent him off! See you when I get back, ginger Cousins.'

Chapter 18

CHARLIE

It's another hot day. Here I am, drawing pictures in the sand with Zak of all people! We've just had a race in the sea and I won by a metre. Zak says I'm a brilliant swimmer and I must say, he's not bad either.

Mum and Cass are playing with Dan. It's so weird, being back in Shipwreck Bay without Dad but I have to say, Zak's more fun in a way. I suppose he's younger and more energetic and he's sort of more encouraging about things. But I guess I could get tired of his jokes!

I came to please Mum and Cass but also, I wanted to get away to the seaside. All this fuss at Cleremont with reporters and so on has upset Gran so she's shutting the shop this weekend and Dad will take her and Freddy out for a drive to their favourite places. I think an apiary (that's where they keep bees) is on the list! I hope she gets back to being a bit more like a softer version of Granite Gran; at the moment she's gone all old and crumbly and it doesn't suit her.

I can see Mum's happy with Zak and Cass and I just have to get used to Mum and Dad splitting up. We think Dad's probably got a girlfriend to do with work so we might have to get used to another change, one day.

'What are you drawing?' Zak asks, finishing his dragon.

'A Husky dog,' I said, giving the tail a good curl with my stick.

'Looks good but where's the sleigh?'

I didn't answer. I was remembering yesterday. Jack came over and said the Police had taken all their tape away and he wondered if we'd go back with him to the island to celebrate. 'Dad and Mum are going around hand in hand and I feel a bit of a spare part,' he said. 'They're going to open the Park again next week, after the Police have released James's body for the funeral. We'll probably open more often because so many people want to come to Cleremont but Dad's not going to let them come to the island. And there's a chance now we may get some sort of grant so we might be able to keep the house. Fingers crossed.'

Cass wasn't keen to go back when I asked her. 'Supposing we see the ghosts again?' she said.

'We won't,' I promised and I was quite sure of that.

The bridge had been roughly repaired now and we walked over to the island. It was one of those heavy days again, when it feels as if the trees are resting, ready for the autumn.

I jumped as the heron rose from the old landing-stage by the clearing, with a loud call. He wheeled overhead, then another heron rose from the other side of the lake and the two birds flew over the island.

'They're right on track,' Jack said. 'Two herons. Family crest, you know.'

Everything was the same except for a lot of footprints

in the clearing and a bit of left-over Police tape tied to the door of the mausoleum.

I'd brought a bunch of Gran's pink dahlias with me. I put them on Wolf's grave. Maybe a bone would have been better but Jack's dogs, who'd come with us, would have stolen it.

Jack and Cass stood by me. 'I wish I'd thought of that,' Jack said unexpectedly. 'I'd like to have known Wolf.' Cass smiled at me.

We sat down, passing round a can of Coke. The spaniels plunged happily into the water after sticks Jack threw.

'You said you saw a dog, didn't you?' Jack asked. 'And a man and a girl...' He shook his head. 'I don't believe in ghosts.' He didn't sound at all sure.

Then he said, 'There's rather a horrible bit I didn't tell you. They found scratch marks on the inside of the door to the mausoleum. They think James wasn't quite dead when he was shoved inside.'

'And he cried out for help.' Cass looked upset. 'Maybe he lived on several days in that horrible place.'

'James is going to be buried next to his mother, in the mausoleum,' Jack said. 'With a proper service beforehand.'

'He must have missed her so much,' Cass said with a jerk in her voice. 'Specially as they were so young when she died and their father...' she tailed off.

'Yeah,' Jack said and we were all silent for a while.

*

127

Now, at Shipwreck Bay, I finished my picture of Wolf and ran through the waves for a last swim. Lying on my back beyond the surf, I remembered how Jack's dogs had suddenly swum back and rushed round the island, sniffing in circles, their tails wagging with excitement. 'A rabbit or something, I guess,' Jack said.

I looked round. Wolf ran out of the bushes and stood, looking at us with those strange blue eyes.

'Look!' I said.

Merry and Magic ran back but they went to sit by Jack.

'What are they looking at?' he said.

He'd be upset that he couldn't see Wolf too. 'I expect it was a rabbit,' Cass and I said at the same time.

I'm treading water. I can see Zak carrying Dan and Mum's calling me for the picnic. And now Cass is wading out to me, bracing against the waves. I'd better go back in case she tries more than two strokes in that surf.

I reach her just as a wave breaks over her. 'Lunatic!' I say, hoiking her out.

She spits out water. 'It's great you came,' she says.

'I wanted to,' I shouted against the surf.

We're the Twins again.

FAMILY TREES

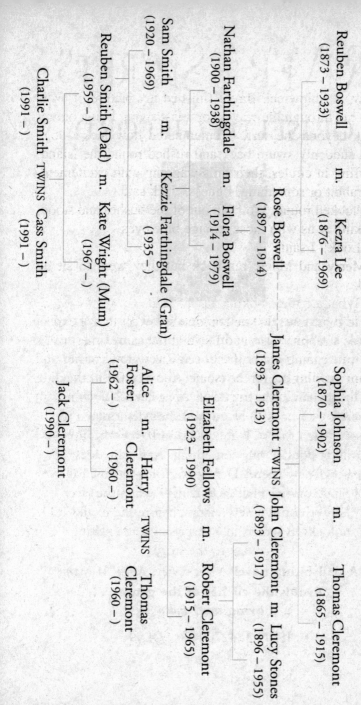

THE TWINS' FAMILY

Reuben Boswell
(1873 – 1933)

m.

Kezra Lee
(1876 – 1969)

Rose Boswell
(1897 – 1914)

Nathan Farthingdale
(1900 – 1938)

m.

Flora Boswell
(1914 – 1979)

Sam Smith
(1920 – 1969)

m.

Kezzie Farthingdale (Gran)
(1935 –)

Reuben Smith (Dad)
(1959 –)

m. Kate Wright (Mum)
(1967 –)

Charlie Smith
(1991 –)

TWINS

Cass Smith
(1991 –)

CLEREMONT FAMILY

Sophia Johnson
(1870 – 1902)

m.

Thomas Cleremont
(1865 – 1915)

James Cleremont
(1893 – 1913)

TWINS

John Cleremont
(1893 – 1917)

m. Lucy Stones
(1896 – 1955)

Elizabeth Fellows
(1923 – 1990)

m.

Robert Cleremont
(1915 – 1965)

Alice Foster
(1962 –)

m.

Harry Cleremont
(1960 –)

TWINS

Thomas Cleremont
(1960 –)

Jack Cleremont
(1990 –)

RIVER of SECRETS

GRISELDA GIFFORD

Fran is very upset because her mother has remarried
and she has to live with her stepfather and his son
at her gran's old home. She was very fond of her
gran, who has recently been found dead in the
nearby river. Was her death an accident? Fran is
sure someone is to blame and she's determined to
solve the mystery. Is the weird girl, Fay, who lives
next door, hiding something? And why does
another new friend, Denny, warn her against Fay's
strange magic? Fran faces danger when the river
almost claims a new victim, before she finally
unlocks its secrets in a surprising and exciting
climax to the story.

'**A nail-biting novel**' 4 star review, *Mizz Magazine*
'**Avoids the clichés of the genre . . .
a moving tale.**' *Independent*

ISBN 1842700456   £4.99

SECOND SIGHT

Griselda Gifford

Jo and her family have just moved to a cramped
inner city flat. She is beaten up by the bullies in her
new school, and her home life is just as difficult.
Her little brother Doddy was rendered speechless in
a car accident and her mother was also injured.
Then Doddy buys a mysterious Eye at the bazaar,
which gives anyone holding it the gift of second
sight. Jo now has the power to solve her
problems – but does she really want to use
the knowledge that she gains?

'Jo is an appealing narrative voice and the novel will
appeal to girls of 10–13 who enjoy fiction based on
relationships.' *School Librarian*

ISBN 1842702173   £4.99